Mary Peplow and De
and travel writers. The
now live there. Their
topics from art history
walking to window sho

By the same authors

The London Fun Book
Edinburgh for Free
My Visit to Edinburgh
Dublin for Free
Glasgow for Free
The Other Museum Guide
Tube Trails

MARY PEPLOW
AND DEBRA SHIPLEY

London for Free

GRAFTON BOOKS

A Division of the Collins Publishing Group

LONDON GLASGOW
TORONTO SYDNEY AUCKLAND

Grafton Books
A Division of the Collins Publishing Group
8 Grafton Street, London W1X 3LA

Third Revised Edition published by Grafton Books 1988
First published in Great Britain by
Panther Books 1984
Reprinted 1985

Copyright © Mary Peplow and Debra Shipley 1984, 1986, 1988

ISBN 0-586-20331-1

Printed and bound in Great Britain by
Collins, Glasgow

Set in Times

To our Grandmothers

Cath Shipley
Cynthia Peplow
Evelyn Saunders

Contents

Preface

'Can you do anything for free these days?' asked dubious friends when we told them we were writing a guidebook to free London. Well, we hope that *London for Free* answers their questions by giving just a taster of how much you can see and do for free in London.

Every day we're growing more and more fond of our Capital City, more amused by its quirky history, more enchanted by its streets and more excited about its future, and every day we're learning something new. How true that famous saying by Dr Samuel Johnson: 'When a man is tired of London he's tired of life; for there is in London all that life can afford.' We found walking the streets of London a fascinating adventure. Everywhere we looked was something to catch the eye and excite the mind – and gradually we fitted together the pieces of the jigsaw to make our own personal picture of this great city.

But we despair when we think of all the things we haven't included, and that's where you can help us. If you've discovered something you can do or see for free in London which you'd like to share with others, then please let us know. Our thanks for the suggestions we've already received which have been included in this third edition. Also, although the times, addresses and telephone numbers were correct at the time of going to press, if you find anything has changed, then we'd be grateful to hear from you.

You may question why we've included some places, such as Marble Hill House and the Ford Motor Company, which are technically outside London, but as they're all so easily accessible by London Transport or British Rail, we felt we'd like to tell you about them. We should also add that in most cases we've given you the nearest tube station, as this is often the easiest way of travelling for newcomers to London; however, if this is some distance away then we've added bus routes and main-line stations. You can pick up free guides to bus, tube and train services within the Greater London area from most tube stations and also from Travel Information Centres at Victoria, Piccadilly Circus, King's Cross, Euston, Oxford Circus, St James's Park and Heathrow tube stations. For help with planning your route, telephone: 01-222 1234 and ask the staff manning London Transport's 24-hour Travel Information Service.

If you need help with any other aspect of your exploration of London, contact the London Tourist Board and Convention Bureau Information Service, telephone 01-730 3488 (there is an automatic queuing system), or drop into one of their tourist offices:

National Tourist Information Centre
Victoria Station Forecourt, SW1
Open: daily, 0900–2030 (1900 during winter months)

Clerkenwell Heritage Centre (Islington Visitor Centre)
33 St John's Square, EC1 Tel: 01-250 1039
Open: April–September, daily, 0900–1800 (weekends 1400–1700), October–March, Monday–Friday, 0900–1700

Croydon Tourist Information Centre
Katharine Street, Croydon, Surrey
Tel: 01-760 5630 or 01-858 6376 ext. 2984/5

Open: Monday, 0930–1900, Tuesday–Friday,
      0930–1800, Saturday, 0900–1700

Greenwich Tourist Information Centre
52–4 Greenwich Church Street, SE10 Tel: 01-858 6376
Open: Easter–mid July, 1000–1700,
      mid July–end September, 1000–1800,
      October–end February, 1000–1600,
      March–Easter, 1000–1700

Harrods Tourist Information Desk
Harrods, Knightsbridge, SW1
Open: during store hours

Harrow Tourist Information Centre
Civic Centre, Station Road, Harrow, Middlesex
Tel: 01-863 5611 ext. 2102/2103
Open: Monday–Friday, 0930–2000, Saturday,
      0930–1700

Heathrow Tourist Information Centres
Heathrow Central Station, Heathrow Airport,
Middlesex
Open: daily, 0900–1800

H.M. Tower of London Tourist Information Centre
West Gate, H.M. Tower of London, EC3
Open: April–October, daily, 1000–1800

Hillingdon Tourist Information Centre
Central Library, High Street, Uxbridge, Middlesex
Tel: Uxbridge (0895) 50600
Open: Monday–Friday, 0930–2000, Saturday,
      0930–1700

Kingston-upon-Thames Tourist Information Centre

Heritage Centre, Fairfield West, Kingston-upon-
Thames, Surrey
Tel: 01-546 5386
Open: Monday–Saturday, 1000–1700

Lewisham Tourist Information Centre
Borough Mall, Lewisham Centre, SE13
Tel: 01-318 5421/2
Open: Monday–Friday, 0915–1715

Richmond Tourist Information Centre
Old Town Hall, Whittaker Avenue, Richmond, Surrey
Tel: 01-940 9125
Open: Monday, Tuesday, Thursday, Friday,
        1000–1800, Saturday, 1000–1700,
        Wednesday, 1000–2000, Sunday, 1015–1615
        (1515 in winter months)

Selfridges Tourist Information Centre
Selfridges, Oxford Street, W1
Open: during store hours

Tower Hamlets Tourist Information Centre
88 Roman Road, E2 Tel: 01-980 3749
Open: Monday–Friday, 0900–1700

Twickenham Tourist Information Centre
District Library, Garfield Road, Twickenham,
Middlesex Tel: 01-892 0032
Open: Monday, Thursday, Friday, 1000–1800,
        Tuesday, 1000–2000, Wednesday, Saturday,
        1000–1700

We hope you'll share our enthusiasm for all that makes
up free London.

CHAPTER ONE
Entertainment

ALBANY EMPIRE THEATRE, Douglas Way, SE8
Tel: (Box Office) 01-691 3333

The Albany Empire, a purpose-built theatre space inside a community complex, is a thriving venue for popular culture. It regularly presents music, theatre and dance. For most of the performances there's a charge, but some previews are free and well worth seeing.

British Rail: New Cross
Details: telephone the box office

EXTRA ... EXTRA ... Beside the Albany Empire you'll find New Cross Market – the place for bargains in household goods. This is very much a market for local people with all sorts of everyday items from plastic buckets to greeting cards on sale. There are plenty of fresh fruit and vegetables at low prices and a small selection which is like a jumble sale with second-hand clothes and bric-à-brac laid out on the pavement.
Open: Wednesday, Friday, Saturday, 0900–1600.

AFRICA CENTRE, 38 King Street, WC2
Tel: 01-836 1973

Delicious spicy smells tempt passers-by into the Africa
Centre. Fronted by a shop selling African wares and with
a popular café specializing in African dishes, the centre is
a focus for all sorts of cultural activities and events from
jazz concerts (fee) to talks on the effects of foreign aid on
Somalia. It also has a bookshop and a good small gallery
which presents an unusual variety of exhibitions.

Tube: Leicester Square
Open: Monday–Friday, 1000–1730, Saturday, 1100–1600

EXTRA . . . EXTRA . . . For a sample of another
national culture make for the Swiss Centre in nearby
Leicester Square. In particular, listen out for the traditional bells which ring out as part of a mechanical display
on the façade of the centre.

BARBICAN CENTRE, Barbican, EC2
Tel: 01-638 4141

This centre, opened in March 1982 by the Queen, boasts
130,000 cubic metres of concrete – enough to build over
19 miles of six-lane motorway! And although your initial
impression may well be one of a huge concrete jungle, if
you take a deep breath and sit down with one of the free
welcoming brochures then you'll soon be able to find your
way around the complex and discover all there is to do on
the different levels. There are free lectures, concerts and
exhibitions, and although membership of the library is

only open to people living, working and studying in the City, you're welcome to browse. It's also worth taking advantage of their clean, well-kept toilets. If you do get lost then don't be afraid to ask for help – you won't be the first nor the last person to do so!

Tube: Moorgate, St Paul's, Barbican, Liverpool Street
Open: Monday–Saturday, 0900–2300,
     Sunday, 1200–2300

EXTRA . . . EXTRA . . . Opposite is the ancient church of St Giles, Cripplegate. Oliver Cromwell was married in the church and the explorer Martin Frobisher regularly worshipped here. William Shakespeare was also a famous visitor. The church is open daily except Saturdays.

BUSKING, COVENT GARDEN, WC2

Once a busy vegetable and flower market, Covent Garden has become a major tourist attraction (*see Covent Garden, page 80, and Jubilee Market, page 84*). The carefully restored cobblestones evoke an atmosphere unique in London and provide a perfect setting for busking and street theatre. The main venue for these often colourful activities is outside St Paul's Church, but under the covered stall area there is a space with benches reserved mainly for musical acts. All the acts are of a very high standard – no one performs without an audition – and are greatly appreciated by the large crowds which quickly gather. (*See also Punch and Judy Festival, page 227*)

Tube: Covent Garden
Time: Daily, best around lunchtime

EXTRA . . . EXTRA . . . Covent Garden has always been
linked historically with the Royal Opera House, better
known as Covent Garden Theatre. It's a huge building
with seats for an audience of 2,154.

CHURCH MUSIC

Many of the City churches organize lunchtime music,
including organ recitals, hi-fi recordings and chamber
music of a very high standard. They usually attract a
regular audience of city workers, and the atmosphere can
sometimes be rather 'clubby'. But don't be put off, as
everyone is more than welcome. For up-to-date details of
times and programmes contact the City of London Information Centre, St Paul's Churchyard, EC4. Tel: 01-
606 3030. Here are just a few of the churches providing
lunchtime entertainment:

All Hallows-by-the-Tower, Byward Street, EC3 (*see page
33*). **Tube:** Tower Hill
Holy Sepulchre, Holborn Viaduct, EC1. **Tube:** St Paul's
St Bride's Church, Fleet Street, EC4 (*see page 55*). **Tube:**
Blackfriars
St Lawrence Jewry, Gresham Street, EC2 (*see page 58*).
Tube: Bank
St Mary-le-Bow, Cheapside, EC2 (*see page 61*). **Tube:**
Bank, St Paul's
St Mary Woolnoth, Lombard Street, EC3 (*see page 62*).
Tube: Bank
St Olave, Hart Street, EC3. **Tube:** Tower Hill
Southwark Cathedral, Cathedral Street, SE1 (*See page
66*). **Tube:** London Bridge

EXTRA . . . EXTRA . . . In the 17th century, the City of London was recognized as the centre for bell-ringing (or campanology, to give it the formal title) and many ringing societies were formed. Today, the only club is the Ancient Society of College Youths who can be heard ringing the bells of St Paul's Cathedral (*see page 64*) every Sunday.

DEGREE AND DIPLOMA ART EXHIBITIONS

One way to see how the world of art is developing is to take a look at work produced by final-year art and design students. Each summer exhibitions of sculpture, ceramics, interior design, stage design, printing and fine art are held at colleges across the capital. Some of the best include:

Central School of Art and Design, Southampton Row, WC1. **Details:** Tel: 01-405 1825 **Tube:** Holborn

Chelsea School of Art, Manresa Road, SW3. **Details:** Tel: 01-749 3236 **Tube:** Sloane Square

City and Guilds of London Art School, 124 Kennington Park Road, SE11. **Details:** Tel: 01-735 2306 **Tube:** Kennington

Kingston Polytechnic, Knights Park, Kingston Upon Thames, Surrey. **Details:** Tel: 01-549 6151 ext 250. **British Rail:** Kingston

London College of Furniture, 81-7 Commercial Road, E1. **Details:** Tel 01-247 1953 **Tube:** Aldgate East

London College of Printing, Elephant and Castle, SE1. **Details:** Tel 01-735 8484 **Tube:** Elephant and Castle

Royal College of Art, Kensington Gore, SW7. **Details:**
  Tel 01-584 5020 **Tube:** High Street Kensington
St Martin's School of Art, 107 Charing Cross Road,
  WC2. **Details:** Tel 01-437 0611 ext 202 **Tube:**
  Tottenham Court Road

EXTRA . . . EXTRA . . . Look out for a booklet called
Galleries, it's free from hotels, restaurants and galleries
including the Tate (*see page 136*). In it you'll find lists of
London's private galleries organized area by area with
helpful maps and information about current exhibitions.

GUILDHALL SCHOOL OF MUSIC AND DRAMA, Barbican, Silk Street entrance, EC2. Tel: 01-628 2571

The Guildhall School moved from its former site in
Blackfriars to the Barbican in 1977. Despite the subse-
quent opening of the prestigious Barbican Centre – home
of the London Symphony Orchestra and Royal Shakespeare Company – the School isn't really over-shadowed
by its glamorous neighbours. The standard of student
work is as high as ever and it's worth going to one of their
lunchtime or evening lectures and recitals arranged by
and for the students. Call in at the main entrance in Silk
Street, EC2, for a free programme of events; complimen-
tary tickets are issued 14 days before a performance.

Tube: Barbican, Moorgate, Liverpool Street, St Paul's
Open: Monday–Friday, 0800–2100, Saturday, 0800–1500

***EXTRA* ... *EXTRA* ...** Students who have passed through Guildhall School include such famous names as Fred Astaire, Noël Coward, Julia McKenzie and Peter Cushing.

LYRIC THEATRE, King Street, Hammersmith, W6.
Tel: 01-741 2311

Every Saturday lunchtime (1230–1430) there's a jazz session in the main foyer with different musicians playing each week. The standard varies but there's always a good audience of jazz fans. The bar and restaurant are open for drinks and snacks. Exhibitions of art and photographs are held regularly in the main foyer and also on the stalls and circle level.

Tube: Hammersmith
Open: daily, 1000–2230

***EXTRA* ... *EXTRA* ...** The present Hammersmith Bridge replaces one built in 1824–7. Designed by William Tierney, it was the first suspension bridge in London. There's a memorial to Tierney in St Paul's Church, Queen Caroline Street, Hammersmith.

MORRIS DANCING

You can't help but feel a spring in your step as you watch the traditional dances performed by Morris Dancers to the music of a fiddle or concertina. Dressed in traditional costume of white shirt, trousers tied at the knee, hats, waistcoats and buckled shoes, they dance at shows and fairs and give displays outside pubs and in open squares. You'll always find them outside Westminster Abbey in Broad Sanctuary, SW1, on Wednesday evenings during the summer months.

Date, time and place: Tel: 01-730 3488 (London Tourist Board and Convention Bureau)

EXTRA . . . EXTRA . . . Morris Dances, performed by Morris groups all over the country, are ancient fertility rites. Dating back well before the 15th century, these dances were supposed to ward off evil spirits and bring fertility to the land. Why Morris? Well, the word probably originates from the Moorish language and means 'strange'. But strange or not these Morris Dancers with their handkerchiefs, sticks and bells certainly add a bit of colour to their surroundings.

MUSEUM/ART GALLERY LECTURES, FILMS AND TALKS

Many museums and art galleries have free activities including guided tours, talks, films and lectures. Most of these often extremely interesting events are timed to fit in with office lunch hours and usually no one minds if you munch a sandwich. Contact the museum or gallery of your choice for more information. The museums below have regular events:

British Museum: Tel: 01-636 1555 (*see page 99*)
Horniman Museum: Tel: 01– 699 2339 (*see page 112*)
Imperial War Museum: Tel: 01-735 8922 (*see page 113*)
Museum of London: Tel: 01-600 3699 (*see page 121*)
Museum of Mankind: Tel: 01-437 2224/8 (*see page 122*)
National Army Museum: Tel: 01-730 0717 (*see page 124*)
National Gallery: Tel: 01-839 3321 (*see page 125*)
Tate Gallery: Tel: 01-821 1313 (*see page 136*)
Victoria and Albert Museum: Tel: 01-589 6371 ext. 429 (*see page 136*)
Whitechapel Art Gallery: Tel: 01-377 0107 (*see page 138*)

EXTRA . . . EXTRA . . . For other ideas on what to do contact local Town Hall, Recreation and Leisure Departments (address in the telephone book).

NATIONAL THEATRE, South Bank, SE1.
Tel: 01-633 0880 (*see also Walk 3, page 247*)

You can spend many a happy hour wandering around the National Theatre. There are exhibitions of work including paintings, posters, photographs, cartoons and stage design in the foyer on all levels. On Saturday lunchtimes and every evening, an hour before the performance, the Lyttelton foyer is packed with people listening to the free music. You can even take your own sandwich supper.

Tube: Waterloo
Open: Lyttelton and Olivier foyers: Monday–Saturday,
1000–2300
Cottesloe foyer: 2 hours before performance

EXTRA . . . EXTRA . . . Shakespeare's famous 'Globe
Playhouse' stood on a site in Bankside, SE1, ten minutes'
walk from the National Theatre, from 1598 until it was
burned down in 1613 during a performance of *Henry VIII*.
This was where many of Shakespeare's plays were given
their first showing.

OPEN-AIR ART EXHIBITIONS

You can spend many a sunny afternoon looking at the
open-air art exhibitions in London. Hopeful painters put
their work on display but there's no compulsion to buy.
You'll also see pavement artists and portrait artists working around these display areas. The places to go are:

Green Park   Along the railings on the Piccadilly side
Tube: Green Park
Weekends
Hampstead   Heath Street
Tube: Hampstead, Golders Green
Weekends (June–August)
Hyde Park   Along the railings on the Bayswater Road
side
Tube: Marble Arch, Lancaster Gate
Sundays
Richmond   The Terrace

Tube: Richmond
Weekends (May and June)
Victoria Embankment Gardens
Tube: Charing Cross, Embankment
Daily in May

EXTRA ... EXTRA ... You'll find an open-air art
exhibition with a difference in Cloth Court, EC1. Look
up at the window of 43 Cloth Fair (in Cloth Court) and
you'll see the painting of a happy family scene. This
painting by Brian Thomas was done to replace the previous blacked-in window and give the chartered surveyors
working in the offices opposite a brighter view. Look out
too for London's colourful murals.

PARK BANDS

Park bands never seem to alter and their starchy formality
makes lounging in a deck-chair positively luxurious! The
bands change regularly – Royal Engineers, Scots Guards,
Royal Green Jackets – but the atmosphere remains the
same. There are performances in the major parks most
days during the summer, including Sundays and Bank
Holidays, so take a stroll down to your local park. Band
performances in the Royal Parks – St James's, Kensington
Gardens, Regent's Park, Hyde Park, Greenwich Park –
are particularly good.

EXTRA ... EXTRA ... When the music's over, take
time to walk through the park and do a bit of bird-

spotting. Magpies, crows, kestrels, sparrows, starlings, gulls and larks – you'll find them all in London's parks.

PUBLIC LIBRARIES

To join one of the hundreds of libraries in London's boroughs and actually borrow books and records you need to prove you live, work or study in the area. However, everyone is free to spend a few minutes or a whole day in the warmth reading the books, magazines and newspapers, or enjoying the talks and activities provided by the different libraries. The staff are always willing to help you find what you're looking for, but do remember that they like to keep the noise down. To find the addresses and facilities offered by libraries look in the *Directory of London Public Libraries*. For specialist libraries look in the directory compiled by the Association of Specialist Libraries and Information Bureaux. These two directories should be available in the reference section of any public library.

EXTRA . . . EXTRA . . . One specialist library worth a mention is the St Bride Printing Library housed in the St Bride Institute, Bride Lane, EC4 (Tel: 01-353 4660). Here you can see an original wooden printing press dated about 1800. If you ask the librarian he'll explain exactly how it used to work.

RIVERSIDE STUDIOS, Crisp Road, Hammersmith, W6. Tel: 01-741 2251

Though, as its name suggests, Riverside Studios is situated beside the river (*see Hammersmith Bridge to Barnes Bridge Footpath, page 155*), it doesn't unfortunately have a waterfront view. Housed in an ex-BBC studio – a decidedly introverted space with no natural light whatsoever reaching the main public areas – Riverside is, however, a major arts venue. The theatre (fee) presents some of the best avant-garde productions in London and has a particularly good reputation for its dance events. There's also a gallery which each month shows a new selection of modern works of art. The walls of the large foyer area (which has a self-service food counter and bar) are also pressed into use for displaying modern paintings. And you can occasionally see a special exhibition in the rehearsal room, for example, work by the Society of British Stage Designers.

Tube: Hammersmith
Open: daily 1200–2300

EXTRA ... EXTRA ... Nearby on Hammersmith Broadway is the Hammersmith Odeon (fee). Once a large cinema, today the Odeon is a popular live music venue which often plays host to international bands.

ROYAL FESTIVAL HALL, Belvedere Road, SE1.
Tel: 01-928 3002 (*see also Walk 3, Page 247*)

There's jazz in the café every Friday, Saturday and Sunday evening at 2000 with a varied programme of music. But do get there early as it's often hard to find a seat. There's also music in the main foyer at lunchtime, and a series of exhibitions on all levels. The bookshop is worth a browse, and there are often signing sessions with famous authors. Even if you're not a music lover, you'll find plenty to do here and no pressure to rush your visit. Indeed, the staff are really rather proud of all their free facilities.

Tube: Waterloo
Open: daily, 1000–2230

EXTRA . . . EXTRA . . . Stroll down The Queen's Walk, SE1, to The South Bank Lion at the foot of Westminster Bridge. This lion, carved out of Coade stone, used to be the mascot of the Lion Brewery in the 19th century. Now it's the mascot of the South Bank. Incidentally, the secret formula used by a factory in Lambeth to make this hard-wearing Coade stone has now been lost.

ROYAL SOCIETY OF ARTS LECTURES,
8 John Adam Street, WC2. Tel: 01-930 5115

Fascinating lectures are given for members of the Royal Society of Arts on a broad range of topical themes: art and architecture; science and technology; industry and commerce; the media, etc. Non-members are made welcome at lectures whenever space is available. Admission is by ticket, obtainable without charge from the Secretary of the Society, as is a lecture programme for each season (October–June).

Tube: Charing Cross

EXTRA . . . EXTRA . . . Nearby in Carting Lane, Strand, WC2, is one of the last examples of a sewer gas lamp in London. Dating from around 1900, the lamp, it is rumoured, burns up gases from the Savoy Hotel sewers below.

SPEAKERS' CORNER, junction of Bayswater Road and Park Lane, Hyde Park, W1

This little corner of Hyde Park, opposite Marble Arch, has been a forum for free speech since 1872. It's great fun to stand and listen to the speakers as they hold forth on subjects from religion and politics to health. It's best to go on Saturday or Sunday afternoon when it's busiest. And if you've got something to say, then there's nothing stopping you!

Tube: Marble Arch

EXTRA . . . EXTRA . . . Idi Amin, former President of Uganda, was a regular in the crowd when he served with the British Army, so keep your eyes open for future notorious statesmen!

TICKETS FOR TELEVISION AND RADIO SHOWS

It's great fun to be part of a live audience for a television or radio show. As well as actually seeing your favourite personalities live, you get to know what really happens during filming. The waiting list is often long, so write for tickets well in advance. You can specify your favourite programme but usually you have to take what comes. Remember, you are only invited to radio and television shows which have a live audience. Write enclosing a stamped addressed envelope to:

Ticket Unit, BBC Broadcasting House, WIA 1AA
         (Radio)
         BBC Television Centre, W12 7RJ
         (Television)

Ticket Office, Thames Television, 149 Tottenham Court
         Road, W1 (Television only)

Ticket Office, London Weekend Television, South
         Bank, Television Centre, SE1 (Television
         only)

EXTRA . . . EXTRA . . . A British inventor, John Logie Baird, was a pioneer in the world of television. In the 1920s he used to experiment with a machine held together with glue, sealing wax and string from his home in Frith Street, W1.

CHAPTER TWO

Historic and Architectural Interest

ALL HALLOWS-BY-THE-TOWER, Byward Street, EC3

Totally gutted in 1941, there is still a lot to see in this pretty church. Saxons built the first church on this site over a Roman Villa (mosaic remains can be seen in the crypt by special request). Many of the memorials in the church have close connections with the sea and take unusual forms. Interesting too is the font known as 'The Tunnellers' Font', a memorial to the Royal Engineers. (*See Church Music, page 18*)

Tube: Tower Hill
Open: Monday–Friday, 0830–1800 (1930 Thursday),
Weekends, 1000–1800

EXTRA . . . EXTRA . . . Samuel Pepys climbed the church tower to get a view of the Great Fire of London, until, as he writes, he 'became afeared to stay there long' and came down again as fast as he could.

ALL SOULS, Langham Place, W1

The BBC morning service comes live from All Souls, which stands next door to BBC Broadcasting House. It was designed by Nash and completed in 1824 as part of

his Regent Street town planning scheme. With its circular
portico of tall pillars and its slender, fluted spire you'll
find the church looks exactly the same from all angles.
The inside has been beautifully restored and modernized
after bomb damage in World War II.

Tube: Oxford Circus
Open: daily 0900–2100 (Saturday 1300)

EXTRA . . . EXTRA . . . Cavendish Square, W1, is just
a short walk away. Laid out in 1717, this square has been
the residence of many notables. Among these is the
painter George Romney (1734–1802), famed for his portrait of Emma, Lady Hamilton.

BIG BEN, The Palace of Westminster, SW1 (*see also
Walk 4, page 251*)

When talking about Big Ben most people are referring to
the whole clock tower on the north-west corner of the
Palace of Westminster (*see Houses of Parliament, page
184*). However, Big Ben is really the hour bell inside. The
bell, which weighs over 13 tons and measures 9 feet in
diameter, is probably named after Sir Benjamin Hall,
First Commissioner of Works, although another story
claims that it was Ben Caunt, a Victorian prize-fighter,
who gave it his name. The clock tower, complete with
clock and bell, was finished in 1858–9. The clock is always
accurate – never more than four seconds slow. The light
above it shines when the House of Commons is sitting.

Tube: Westminster

EXTRA . . . EXTRA . . . Big Ben was one of the bells re-cast at the Whitechapel Bell Foundry, 34 Whitechapel High Street, E1. A bell is melted down and re-cast when it's out of tune or cracked. The foundry dates back to 1570 and, as the plaques on the wall outside proudly declare, has been at its present site since 1738. The Liberty Bell of America was first cast at the foundry, and all the bells at Westminster Abbey (*see page 70*) have been re-cast here.

BRIXTON WINDMILL, Blenheim Gardens, Brixton, SW2. Tel: 01-671 2907

Brixton Windmill is a real, and very pleasant, surprise; busy Brixton Hill gives no indication that a 19th-century windmill, still in working order, is just a few minutes' walk away. Built in 1816, this splendid structure has now been well preserved and is a popular place with children. There's a helpful plan to show you the functions of the various pieces of machinery, including the wallower, the spur wheel and the bedstone.

Tube: Clapham South, Brixton
Open: times vary throughout the year; it's best to
          telephone before visiting.

EXTRA . . . EXTRA . . . If a place has been called 'Windmill' (e.g. Windmill Street or Windmill Road) it's a fair bet that at some time in the past there was a windmill in the area. The London *A–Z* lists some 23 places which are called 'Windmill'. One of them, Windmill Hill, NW3, dates from the 17th century – a survey of 1680 shows there was a windmill on the site.

BUCKINGHAM PALACE, The Mall, SW1 (*see also Walk 4, page 251*)

Buckingham Palace, one of the capital's top ten tourist attractions, is the London home of the Queen. When she's in residence, the Royal Standard flies from the flagpole on the roof. Queen Victoria was the first monarch to live here, moving in only three weeks after her accession to the throne.

The Palace was built in the early 18th century as a town house for the Duke of Buckingham, but work wasn't completed until 1912 when the front was reconstructed in Portland Stone. This was in keeping with the Mall and the newly erected Victoria Memorial. Don't be deceived by the size of the Palace – it's far bigger than it looks, with State Rooms stretching far back from the frontage. The apartments of the Royal Family are in the North Wing.

Tube: Green Park, Victoria
Open: not open to the public; viewing from the outside only.

EXTRA . . . *EXTRA* . . . The ceremony of the Changing of the Queen's Guards takes place in the front courtyard every day at 1130 in the summer and alternate days in the winter. It lasts about half an hour and you can get a good view through the railings. The Guards come from either the Chelsea Barracks or Wellington Barracks. They leave

Chelsea Barracks at 1045 and march via Ebury Street and Buckingham Gate. From Wellington Barracks they leave at 1100 and march via Birdcage Walk. To check that there is a Guard change telephone: 01-730 3488 (London Tourist Board and Convention Bureau).

BUNHILL FIELDS, City Road, EC1

As the regular path sweeper here likes to tell visitors, 'There ain't much life here.' It's a burial ground for over 120,000 bodies. The moss-covered headstones of John Bunyan, Daniel Defoe and William Blake are among the many that crowd together in this small graveyard. The land, which derives its name from 'Bone Hill', was cordoned off in 1665 as a burial ground for victims of the Great Plague, although it was never used for this purpose. Instead it became a burial ground for non-conformists until it was closed in 1852. The northern section is a lovely, peaceful garden.

Tube: Old Street, Moorgate
Open: Monday–Friday, 0730–1600
      Weekends, 0930–1600

EXTRA . . . EXTRA . . . Opposite is the Chapel of John Wesley, founder of Methodism. His mahogany pulpit is in the centre. Wesley (1703–91) lived and died in the small house next door and is buried in the churchyard.

ELTHAM PALACE, off Court Yard, SE9. Tel: 01-859 2112

Eltham was once a favourite palace with Kings and Queens; from the time of Henry III to Charles I they settled here with their courts. In 1649 a survey carried out by Parliament described Eltham Palace as a 'Capital Mansion House built of brick, stone and timber'. It went on to list numerous rooms, apartments, servants' quarters, a chapel and hall. Today, only the Great Hall (recently restored) survives, but it's a hall with stories to tell and is well worth the trek out of the city centre to see. Its hammer beam roof is particularly dramatic, though perhaps more romantic is the small bridge built by Richard II which still spans the water-filled moat.

British Rail: Eltham
Open: October–April, Thursday and Sunday, 1100–1900.
(This is only a guide, it is best to check in advance with the controllers of the palace – the Army Education Corps – on the above number.)

EXTRA . . . EXTRA . . . All around the palace street names give indications of the area's historic and royal past: Court Road, Kings Orchard, Prince John Road, Archery Road and Tiltyard Approach. Wander down King John's Walk (it passes between the attractive half-timbered Chancellor's Lodgings and the moat) and you'll find yourself in an open meadow with fine views over south London towards the City.

FISHMONGERS' HALL, King William Street, EC4. Tel: 01-626 3531

Home of the Worshipful Company of Fishmongers, this 19th-century hall welcomes visitors on special open days in May, June and July. The Company, the fourth oldest of the livery companies, is one of the few that still carries out its ancient duties which include examining the quality of fish coming into Billingsgate Market (*see page 179*). You'll be taken around the magnificent hall by a well-informed guide who gives details about the Company and points out all the many fascinating features and treasures including Annigoni's first portrait of the Queen.

Tube: Monument, Cannon Street
Open: details available from the City of London Information Centre, St Paul's Churchyard, EC4. Tel: 01-606 3030. Visits can be arranged for other times if you contact the Clerk at Fishmongers' Hall well in advance.

EXTRA . . . EXTRA . . . One of the most renowned members of the Company was William Walworth, a Prime Warden and Lord Mayor of London who is reputed to have saved the life of the young Richard II in 1381 during the Peasants' Revolt in Smithfield Market. Walworth came to the rescue of the king and stabbed his attacker, Wat Tyler, leader of the revolt. The dagger is on show in Fishmongers' Hall.

FREEMASONS' HALL, Great Queen Street, WC2.
Tel: 01-831 9811

Unless you're involved in the Craft of Freemasonry, it's always something of a mystery. Not a lot of people know about the secrets of the society, and few know that Freemasons' Hall, home of the United Grand Lodge of England, is open to the public for guided tours of the temples, library and museum. It's a magnificent and quite awe-inspiring building, with the Grand Temple as the highlight of the visit. Steeped in symbolism from the heavy bronze doors that swing open at the touch of a finger to the black and white flooring, the Grand Temple can be quite overpowering at first, but stand back, enjoy the silent beauty of your surroundings and let your guide explain all. The tour of Freemasons' Hall lasts around an hour and a half and as well as having the chance to experience a truly beautiful building, you'll also gain at least some insight into the world of Freemasonry.

Tube: Holborn, Covent Garden
Open: Tours, Monday–Friday at 1100, 1200, 1400, 1500 and 1600. Saturdays by arrangement.

EXTRA . . . EXTRA . . . Not far away in Bow Street is the Bow Street Police Station, London's oldest police station, which gave its name to the Bow Street Runners. Note the absence of the traditional blue lamp outside. Apparently, Queen Victoria thought it too near the Royal Opera House for such a vulgar sight!

GOLDSMITHS' HALL, Foster Lane, EC2.

The Worshipful Company of Goldsmiths is one of the
oldest of London's livery companies, dating back to
before 1180. Their rich history is encapsulated in their
Hall, designed by Philip Hardwick and completed in 1835.
It's the fourth Goldsmiths' Hall to stand on this island site
in Foster Lane. There are several free exhibitions held
here during the year, such as the Goldsmiths' Fair, usually
in October. However, the best time to visit the Hall and
enjoy its magnificent collection of goldsmiths' works of
art – ancient and modern – is on one of the six annual
open days. A helpful guide will tell you about the treasures. Don't miss the Roman stone altar dedicated to the
goddess Diana.

Tube: St Paul's
Open: for the dates of open days contact The City of
London Information Centre, St Paul's
Churchyard, EC4. Tel: 01-606 3030

EXTRA . . . EXTRA . . . British silver, gold and platinum
are quality-tested at the Assay Office in Goldsmiths' Hall.
Items found to be up to standard are given a special
hallmark. To find out more about the different hallmarks
and what they mean pick up a free leaflet called quite
simply 'Hallmarks' from Goldsmiths' Hall.

GUILDHALL, Gresham Street, EC2. Tel: 01-606 3030 (*see also Walk 5, page 255*)

Guildhall has been the centre of Civic Government for nearly 1000 years. It is here that the Lord Mayor and Sheriffs are elected every year (*see page 221*), and here that the Lord Mayor's Banquet takes place and the Freedom of the City is presented. As you walk through Guildhall you get a magnificent feeling for the history of the proud building. The crypt, porch and medieval walls, which were built between 1411 and 1440, all survived the Great Fires of 1666 and 1940, and other parts have been carefully restored. The Great Hall, 152 feet long and 40½ feet wide, has seen many important trials, including that of the poet, the Earl of Surrey, for treason in 1547. Indeed, there is so much to discover at Guildhall that it's well worth asking the Beadle on duty for a free guide. Also here, see the Guildhall Library (*page 108*) and Clockmakers' Company Museum (*page 102*).

Tube: Bank, Moorgate, St Paul's, Mansion House
Open: Monday–Friday, 1000–1700

EXTRA . . . EXTRA . . . Nearby toilets in Guildhall Buildings, EC2 – a narrow street off Gresham Street – are another pleasurable aspect of a trip to Guildhall. Highly polished brasswork, flowers and a friendly attendant make a visit a joy!

HABERDASHERS' HALL, Staining Lane, EC2.
Tel: 01-606 0967

A tour of Haberdashers' Hall is a real event – it only happens three times a year! First you're shown into an elegant chandeliered Courtroom and then given an absorbing introduction to the world of the guild – from the days when 'foreigner' was a label applied to anyone from further afield than a three-mile radius of London, to the modern-day guild's charity activities. Then the tour (which lasts about an hour) covers the Committee Room, which is decorated with reproduction 17th-century wallpaper; the Livery Hall, panelled in a very grand manner with English Oak; the Luncheon Room, again panelled but this time finely in pine; and last but not least, the Vault Room – the Haberdashers' treasure trove. Incidentally, *do not* ask about haberdashery; the Company in fact takes its name from the rough woollen cloth worn beneath armour and they're very proud of their origins!

Tube: Bank, St Paul's
Open: only three days per year; for dates and to arrange a tour write well in advance to the Clerk.

EXTRA . . . EXTRA . . . Haberdashers' Company patron saint is St Catherine. She came to a gruesome end (all is explained during the tour) and it's said that the firework called 'Catherine Wheel' is named after the method of her execution. You can see her portrait in the Luncheon Room.

HENRY VIII's WINE CELLAR, Ministry of
Defence, Horse Guards Avenue, SW1. Tel: 01-921 4849

This cellar, now beneath the Ministry of Defence building, was one of the additions that Cardinal Wolsey made
to his palace, York Place, between 1514 and 1529. Henry
VIII moved into York Place in 1529 and renamed it
Whitehall Palace. The cellars were kept stocked with fine
wines and they survived the fire of 1698 which completely
destroyed most of the rest of the Palace. The cellar, which
is 62 feet long, 32 feet wide and 20 feet high, is a vaulted
undercroft with ten bays and four octagonal pillars. You'll
find this atmospheric little crypt at the end of a maze of
rather bleak corridors – a welcome and historic relief.

Tube: Westminster, Charing Cross, Embankment
Open: Tours Saturdays only, April–September, 1430–
1630. Apply in writing to: Department of the
Environment, Property Services Agency, Room
10/14, St Christopher House, Southwark Street,
EC1

EXTRA . . . EXTRA . . . When Queen Mary visited the
wine cellar in the 1930s she said she hoped it would be
preserved – so a preservation order was passed. But when
Horse Guards Avenue was widened, the cellar had to be
moved. And so in 1949, the whole cellar, weighing 1000
tons, was moved 43 feet across, lowered 18 feet 9 inches
and then rolled back 33 feet 10 inches – without a stone
being removed.

HIGHGATE CEMETERY, Swains Lane, Highgate, N6. Tel: 01-340 1834 (*see also Walk 6, page 257*)

The cemetery lies on either side of Swains Lane. The eastern part is best known for the grave of Karl Marx, buried in 1883. The western part, just below St Michael's Church, must be one of the eeriest places in London with its catacombs, tombs and vaults. Many of the great Victorians are buried here and the cemetery abounds in legends and stories. Your guide will reveal all . . . Both cemeteries are absolutely fascinating to visit – well worth a trip.

Tube: Archway
Open: Eastern cemetery: April–September
Monday–Saturday, 0900–1700
Sunday, 1400–1700
October–March, Monday–Saturday, 0900–1600
Sunday 1300–1600

Western cemetery (guided tours only):
April–September daily, 1000–1600 on the hour
October–March daily, 1000–1500 on the hour

EXTRA . . . EXTRA . . . Karl Marx first came to England from Germany in 1849 (*see Marx Memorial Library, page 119*) and lived at 28 Dean Street, W1, from 1851 to 1856. The building is now an exclusive Italian restaurant called Leoni's Quo Vadis, but a visitor to Marx's rooms once described them as 'in the worst, therefore also the cheapest, quarters of London. He occupies two rooms . . . in the whole apartment there is not one clean and good piece of furniture to be found; all is broken, tattered and torn, everywhere is the greatest disorder.' Times change!

HORSE GUARDS, Whitehall, SW1 (*see also Walk 4, page 251*)

Horse Guards, now the headquarters of the Commander in Chief of the Home Forces, is built on the site of the old tiltyard of Whitehall Palace. The grey stone building, designed by William Kent in 1760, lies symmetrically around three sides of the forecourt. Through the court-yard and under the central arch is Horse Guards Parade, the largest parade ground in London. This is where the Trooping the Colour takes place on the Queen's official birthday in June.

The Queen's Life Guard keeps up a 24-hour guard outside Horse Guards. The ceremony of the Changing of the Guard, always a colourful event to watch, takes place here at 1100 on Monday–Saturday and 1000 on Sunday and lasts about 25 minutes. The Guards leave Hyde Park Barracks 32 minutes before the ceremony and ride via Hyde Park Corner, Constitution Hill and the Mall. To check the times of the ceremony, telephone 01-730 3488 (London Tourist Board and Convention Bureau).

Tube: Westminster

EXTRA . . . EXTRA . . . Opposite is Banqueting House (entrance fee); a joy to look at. Designed by Inigo Jones in 1619, it's the only building left of the old Palace of Whitehall, the London residence of the monarchs of England from 1529–1698. It's now used for Government receptions.

HOUSE OF ST BARNABAS-IN-SOHO, 1 Greek Street, Soho Square, W1. Tel: 01-437 1894

In the midst of Soho, beside a string of popular restaurants, there survives an 18th-century mansion – St Barnabas-in-Soho. It's the last house in Soho Square to retain its magnificent and exuberant interior decorations. Inside (it can be difficult to get inside – be persistent and keep ringing the bell) you'll be treated to a fascinating guided tour which includes: the main staircase with its original central lantern (now converted for electricity); the Grand Dining Room with its fabulous rococo plasterwork (look out for the two dragons which signify that the first owner of the house, Richard Beckford, was an Alderman of the City of London); the Record Room which still has its original candelabra; and a crinoline staircase – specially designed so that the ladies of the house could walk down the stairs wearing their wide crinoline dresses. An additional treat is the tiny and very beautiful chapel – the foundation stone was laid by Mrs Gladstone in 1862.

Tube: Tottenham Court Road
Open: Wednesday 1430–1615, Thursday 1100–1230. To arrange a visit telephone or write to the Tours Organizer (address above).
Charity donations welcomed

EXTRA . . . EXTRA . . . In the garden behind the house you can see the last surviving mulberry tree planted by the Huguenots for the silk trade, the tree Charles Dickens described in *A Tale Of Two Cities*.

JEWEL TOWER, St Margaret Street, SW1. Tel: 01-222 2219

Though situated opposite the Houses of Parliament (*see page 184*) and beside Westminster Abbey (*see page 70*), very few people seem to discover Jewel Tower. Still partially moated, the tower is the least altered remnant of the medieval palace of Westminster. Inside you can see a very good example of an unrestored 14th-century ribbed vault with grotesque decorative bosses. Jewel Tower takes its name from its original purpose – it was a safe for the king's jewels and plate. It later became a records office for Parliament and later still a weights and measures office. Today visitors can climb a spiral staircase and explore three levels of the tower, which now houses a selection of old measures including an Elizabethan bushel dated 1601. Look out too for an oak-panelled wall plate with elm piles – it once supported the building's face – and a fascinating exhibition of objects found in the moat – there's a pin polisher, pieces of Chinese porcelain and several tooth brushes!

Tube: Westminster
Open: mid March–mid October, Monday–Saturday, 0930–1830; mid October–mid March 0930–1600, (but it often closes at short notice so it's best to telephone in advance).

EXTRA . . . EXTRA . . . Nearby Old Palace Yard is, according to contemporary accounts, the place where Guy Fawkes (*see Firework Night page 231*) and his fellow conspirators were executed on 31 January 1606 – having been brought back from the Tower of London to the scene of their crime.

LONDON ORATORY, Brompton Road, SW7.
Tel: 01-589 4811

Built in heavy Italian Renaissance style in 1884, the London Oratory (also known as the Brompton Oratory) has the third widest nave in England and is the second largest Catholic church in the capital. Particularly interesting are the Lady Altar and the Altar of St Philip Neri; look out too for the statue in the courtyard of Cardinal Newman, who introduced the 'Congregation of the Oratory' to England.

Tube: South Kensington
Open: daily, 0700–2000

EXTRA ... EXTRA ... Broom once grew on open common land through which the busy Brompton Road now passes, hence the name Brompton or 'broom-town'.

LONDON WALL, EC2 (*see also Walk 5, page 255*)

Walk along London Wall, EC2, and look out for the remains of the Roman Wall, built in the 2nd century A.D. It enclosed 330 acres of land and stretched from the east side of the City (where the Tower of London now stands) to Blackfriars. There were gates at Aldersgate, Aldgate, Bishopsgate, Cripplegate, Newgate and Ludgate. In 1415 another gate was added at Moorgate. If you're especially interested in the Roman Wall then it would be worthwhile spending an hour or so at the Museum of London, London Wall, EC2 (*page 121*) and studying their extensive and fascinating exhibition about the Wall.

Tube: St Paul's, Barbican, Moorgate

EXTRA . . . EXTRA . . . The poet John Keats was born in a house on the site of 85 Moorgate, EC2, now a pub called The Moorgate. His father ran livery stables here.

MANSION HOUSE, Wallbrook EC4. Tel: 01-626 2500

This Palladian building is the official residence of the Lord Mayors of London (*see Election of the Lord Mayor, page 221*) during their year of office. It was designed in 1739–53 by George Dance the Elder, and is one of the most pleasing buildings in the City. It's worth a look from the outside even if you don't get inside. But through the doors, it's a story of grandeur and elegance, with the splendid Egyptian Hall and State Drawing Rooms among other opulent rooms. Guided tours only, lasting about one hour.

Tube: Bank, Mansion House
Open: Tours on Tuesday, Wednesday, Thursday, 1100 and 1400. For tickets apply to: Principal Assistant's Office, at the above address.

EXTRA . . . EXTRA . . . Mansion House is built on the site of the old Stocks Market and it was here that the Great Plague broke out in 1665.

MARBLE ARCH, W1

This was originally designed in 1828 by John Nash, on the model of the Arch of Constantine in Rome, as a gateway to Buckingham Palace (*page 36*). However, when it was discovered that it was too narrow for the State Coach, it was moved in 1851 to become the gateway to Hyde Park (*see page 158*). It stands close to the site of the Tyburn Tree, a gallows used for public executions until 1783.

Tube: Marble Arch

EXTRA . . . EXTRA . . . One of the last women to hang in this country was Ruth Ellis in 1955. She shot her boyfriend outside the Magdala Tavern in South Hill Park, NW3. Incidentally, this pub is also famed for its stuffed duck-billed platypus!

MARBLE HILL HOUSE, Richmond Road, Twickenham, Middlesex. Tel: 01-892 5115

This fine Palladian villa stands in its own park near the Orleans House Gallery (*page 129*). It was built for Henrietta Howard, Countess of Suffolk and mistress of George II, between 1724 and 1729. It has been called 'a complete example of an English Palladian villa' and, as such, is worth a visit. It now houses a collection of period furniture and paintings.

Tube: Richmond, then bus 73, 27
Open: February–October, Mondays–Thursdays and
weekends, 1000–1700, November–January,
1000–1600

EXTRA ... EXTRA ... Marble Hill Park is almost
worth visiting in its own right. There are some well laid
out flower beds, trees, and expanses of grass for sport or
gentle walks by the river. Look out for a large black
walnut tree. Planted in the early 18th century, it is said to
be one of the largest in Britain. When last measured in
1979 its vital statistics were: height 92 feet, girth at 4 feet
from the ground 17 feet 6 inches. The park is open from
0700 to dusk.

ORDER OF ST JOHN, St John's Gate, St John's
Lane, Clerkenwell, EC1. Tel: 01-253 6644

St John's Gate belongs to the Order of St John who,
along with the Knights Templar, defended the Christian
Kingdoms in the Holy Land. The Priory at Clerkenwell,
of which St John's Gate is a remain, was the administra-
tive centre in England for the property of the Knights of
St John. The Gatehouse was the main entrance to the
priory and dates back to 1504. After the dissolution it
housed the offices of Elizabeth I's Master of Revels and
in the 18th century was the offices of *Gentleman's Maga-
zine*. Later still it became an inn called The Old Jerusalem
Tavern. Excellent free guided tours of the building
include a visit to the nearby 12th-century crypt. (*See also
the Museum of the Order of St John, page 123*.)

Tube: Farringdon
Open: Tuesday, Friday and Saturday. Tours begin at
1100 and 1430 and take about half an hour.

EXTRA . . . EXTRA . . . A short walk away at 14–16 Farringdon Lane, EC1, is Clerks' Well. This medieval well, which gave its name to the surrounding area of Clerkenwell, was discovered by workmen in 1924 and is thought to be over 1000 years old. It has been restored and now has a viewing gallery and small display of its history. To view contact Clerkenwell Heritage Centre, 33 St John's Square, EC1. Tel: 01-250 1039.

RANGER'S HOUSE, Chesterfield Walk, Blackheath, SE10. Tel: 01-853 0035

This early 18th-century house was the home of Philip, 4th Earl of Chesterfield, famed for his great wit and letters, from 1748 to 1772. Another celebrated person to live here was the Duchess of Brunswick who moved to the house in 1807 so she could be near to Montague House where her daughter, Caroline, Princess of Wales, was living. In 1815 it acquired its name Ranger's House when it became the official residence of the Ranger of Greenwich Park. The house, which is now noted for its long Gallery with the Suffolk Collection of Jacobean and Stuart portraits, was first opened to the public in 1902 as refreshment rooms. (*See also Greenwich Park, page 154, and Blackheath, page 147.*)

Bus: 53
British Rail: Blackheath, Greenwich
Open: daily, 1000–1700 (1600 November–January)

EXTRA . . . EXTRA . . . The *Cutty Sark*, one of the most famous old clippers, is on show at Greenwich Pier.

Although you have to pay to go inside you can get a good look at this old lady of the sea from the outside. Also at the Pier is *Gypsy Moth IV*, which the late Sir Francis Chichester sailed single-handed around the world in 1966–7.

ST BARTHOLOMEW-THE-GREAT, West Smithfield, EC1

A priory was founded here in 1123 by a courtier of Henry I. The priory was entered by the present 13th-century porch – a stone archway with a Tudor-style gatehouse, dating from 1559, built over it. The priory nave extended the whole length of the present churchyard and remains of one side of its cloisters (much restored and rebuilt in the 15th century) can still be seen. The interior is formed from the original Norman choir with vaulted aisles. Look out for an interesting 13th-century coffin and an inscribed book of the Imperial Society of the Knights Bachelor.

Tube: Farringdon, St Paul's, Barbican
Open: Monday–Saturday, 0830–1630, Sunday 0830–2015

EXTRA . . . EXTRA . . . Nearby is Snow Hill, EC1. This hill is rich in history. It was here that John Bunyan died of a cold in 1688 and apparently it's also here that upper-class revellers used to have great fun rolling women down in barrels!

ST BRIDE'S CHURCH, Fleet Street, EC4.

Known as 'The Printer's Church', this popular church, the seventh on the site, has long been associated with journalism and print. Designed by Wren, the spire looks especially beautiful at night when it is floodlit. The crypt has been converted into a fascinating and most atmospheric museum tracing the history of London through the history of the church from Roman times to present day with an amazing array of archaeological finds and relics. It's well worth setting time aside to visit this peaceful church and unusual museum. (*See Church Music, page 18*)

Tube: Blackfriars
Open: daily 0900–1700

EXTRA . . . EXTRA . . . The steeple of St Bride's has been an inspiration for many wedding cakes. Apparently, William Rich, a pastry cook at Ludgate Hill, could see the steeple from his window and used it as a model for his famous wedding cakes in the late 18th century. But don't be misled, that's not how the church got its name – it's because it's dedicated to St Bridget.

ST ETHELDREDA'S, Ely Place, EC1

You may not have seen St Etheldreda's but you may well have heard one of the BBC's many musical recordings made in this historic church. St Etheldreda's is the oldest Catholic church in Britain, dating back to before 1260, and considered one of the finest examples of Gothic architecture in Europe. Indeed, the tracery of the walls and windows is so delicately decorative it almost defies belief. Visitors come from near and far to enjoy the rich history and fine architecture of this unique church and to take part in Sunday Morning Mass which is still sung in Latin by the choir (*see also Blessing the Throats, pages 200–201*).

Tube: Chancery Lane, Farringdon
Open: daily

EXTRA . . . EXTRA . . . Ely Place was once noted for its delicious strawberries. They're even mentioned in Shakespeare's *Richard III*. The Duke of Gloucester says to the Bishop of Ely, 'When I was last in Holborn, I saw good strawberries in your garden there: I do beseech you, send for some of them.' Today, a Strawberrie Fayre is held in Ely Place every June.

ST GEORGE THE MARTYR, Borough High Street, SE1

You could write a book about this 18th-century church. It's really rich in historic and literary connections, but it's probably best known as 'Little Dorrit's Church'. In Dickens's novel *Little Dorrit* the heroine is found asleep on the steps of the church and taken in for the night. It's also at this church that she later marries Arthur Clennam. Look to the stained glass window at the east of the church and you'll see the tiny, innocent figure of Little Dorrit. There's a fascinating story about the church clock too. At night only three of the four faces were lit up. These are the faces which look on to the Borough district. The people of Bermondsey couldn't see the time as their clock face was in darkness. This was because the parishioners here refused to contribute to the Church Appeal!

Tube: Borough
Open: daily except Saturday

EXTRA . . . EXTRA . . . The churchyard is opposite and is dominated by a large plaque stating: 'This site was originally the Marshalsea Prison made famous by the late Charles Dickens in his well known work *Little Dorrit.*' Dickens knew the prison well – he used to visit his father who was imprisoned here for debt. The churchyard is now a peaceful garden.

ST JAMES'S CHURCH, Piccadilly, W1

This lovely Wren church has successfully been kept alive by a huge range of extra-ecclesiastical activity. There's a thriving brass-rubbing centre (fee) and, outside the main entrance, a regular small market of jewellery and souvenirs. The inside of the church is often used for concerts and exhibitions – there always seems to be something happening. When you visit St James's don't forget to look up – there's a beautiful white barrelled ceiling with golden details. The church gardens are also pretty and there are lots of seats.

Tube: Piccadilly Circus, Green Park
Open: Monday–Saturday, 1000–1800, Sunday 1200–1800

EXTRA . . . EXTRA . . . In nearby Piccadilly Circus (look out for the statue of Eros, also known as The Angel of Charity, in the middle of the Circus) there's a new shopping and entertainment complex called the Trocadero. This indoor 'international village', which is full of restaurants and souvenir shops, is home for the Guinness World of Records Exhibition (fee to enter).

ST LAWRENCE JEWRY-NEXT-GUILDHALL, Gresham Street, EC2 (*see also Walk 5, page 255*)

This is the Corporation of London's own church. It was rebuilt by Wren after the Great Fire of 1666 and was one of his most expensive City churches. Completely gutted during World War II it was restored by Cecil Brown and now has a magnificent interior. The best time to visit is on a Tuesday when there is a free organ recital. (*See Church Music, page 18.*)

Tube: Bank, Moorgate, St Paul's
Open: Monday–Friday, 0830–1800, Weekends, 0830–1700

EXTRA . . . EXTRA . . . St Lawrence was killed by being flayed and roasted alive on a gridiron in A.D. 258. A painting illustrating his martyrdom is in the vestibule, and the weather-vane on the spire of the church is in the form of a gridiron in his memory.

ST MARGARET'S, St Margaret Street, SW1

St Margaret's is the parish church of the House of Commons (*see Houses of Parliament, page 184*). It was founded in the 11th or 12th century but was rebuilt in 1504–23 by Robert Stowell, the master mason of Westminster Abbey (*page 70*). Chaucer and Caxton worshipped here and Milton, Pepys and Winston Churchill were married in this lovely church which is dwarfed by Westminster Abbey. Full of interesting detail and tradition – the headless body of Sir Walter Raleigh is said to be buried beneath the High Altar – this church should not be missed.

Tube: Westminster, St James's Park
Open: Monday–Saturday, 0930–1600, Sunday,
      1300–1600

EXTRA . . . EXTRA . . . On the lawn facing Whitehall, and very close to the place where he was beheaded, is a statue of Sir Walter Raleigh (1551–1618), courtier and explorer.

ST MARTIN-IN-THE-FIELDS, Trafalgar Square, WC1

On the corner of busy Trafalgar Square (*page 68*) and just across the road from the National Gallery (*page 125*), you can't miss St Martin-in-the-Fields with its great classical portico and Portland stone steeple. It was designed by James Gibb and completed in 1722. Though not used by the Royal Family, it's the parish church of Buckingham Palace (*page 36*) and above the chancel there's a royal box complete with fireplace. A church has stood on this spot for nearly 800 years. Way back in the 13th century, a tiny chapel was built and dedicated to St Martin of Tours, a helper of the poor – a tradition maintained by the present church which aims to help young people and some of London's homeless.

Tube: Charing Cross, Leicester Square
Open: daily, 0730–2000

EXTRA . . . EXTRA . . . In 1924 the world's first broadcast church service was held at St Martin-in-the-Fields.

ST MARY ABCHURCH, Abchurch Lane, EC4

A solid, square, Wren church built 1681–7, St Mary Abchurch is well worth a visit as much of the original decoration has been retained, including carvings by Grinling Gibbons. The most spectacular aspect of the church is, however, its huge painted dome, which contrasts well with the simple clear-glass windows. The churchyard on the south front has been cobbled in patterns and is a pleasant contrast to busy Cannon Street, particularly in the spring when it is full of daffodils.

Tube: Cannon Street, Mansion House, Monument
Open: Monday–Friday, 1100–1600

EXTRA . . . EXTRA . . . Cannon Street takes its name from the candlemakers who once lived and worked in the area. They were, however, made to move into the country because of complaints about the terrible smell emanating from their candlemaking.

ST MARY-LE-BOW, Cheapside, EC2 (also known as Bow Church)

Only the tower and the steeple of this church designed by Wren and built in 1670–83 survived the fire of 1941. The result is a rather unusual, spacious interior with modern stained glass by John Hayward. The jewel-bright colours of the stained glass contrast very effectively with the simple white walls. Noteworthy too is the modern rood which marks the division between the nave and the chancel. Beneath the church is a Norman crypt (*c.* 1090) which is well worth a visit. It is used for the Court of Arches which decides Ecclesiastical Law cases and confirms the election of Bishops. (*See also Church Music, page 18.*)

Tube: Bank, St Paul's
Open: Monday–Friday

EXTRA . . . EXTRA . . . The 'great bell of Bow' features in the nursery rhyme *Oranges and Lemons*, which is probably at least 500 years old. To be a true 'Cockney' requires being born within earshot of the 'Bow Bells'.

ST MARY-LE-STRAND, Strand, WC2

This baroque gem, designed by James Gibb and built between 1714 and 1717, is marooned in the middle of busy Strand. It is, however, well worth braving the traffic to take a look at its splendid decorative ceiling, subtle stained glass windows, and simple benches, all of which combine in complete harmony. Outside in a tiny garden, defying pollution, flower two magnolia trees, but this is not a place to dwell – the traffic noise is terrible.

Tube: Aldwych
Open: Monday–Friday, daylight hours,
Sunday 1030–1230

EXTRA . . . EXTRA . . . While in the Strand take a look at Gladstone's memorial. The statesman, of whom Queen Victoria complained, 'He speaks to me as if I were a public meeting', is shown in the robes of Chancellor of the Exchequer amid groups expressing Brotherhood, Education, Aspiration and Courage.

ST MARY WOOLNOTH, Lombard Street, EC3

Designed by Wren's pupil Nicholas Hawksmoor, St Mary Woolnoth was built in 1726–7 and has been favoured by some notable people. From the beautifully inlaid pulpit, John Newton, the reformed slave trader, denounced slave-trading and inspired William Wilberforce, a member of his congregation, to fight for its abolition in the House of Commons. There is a memorial to Newton on the north wall. T. S. Eliot mentioned the church's clock in his well-known poem *The Waste Land*:

'. . . To where St Mary Woolnoth kept the hours
With a dead sound on the final stroke of nine . . .'

(*See also Church Music, page 18.*)

Tube: Bank
Open: Monday–Friday, 0900–1645

EXTRA . . . EXTRA . . . When you get off the tube at
Bank, look out for the plaque noting the site of the
General Letter Office (1653–66). Here in 1661 the first
postmarks in the world were struck.

ST PANCRAS STATION, Euston Road, NW1

This is a classic piece of Victorian architecture by Sir
George Gilbert Scott in the Gothic style. The exuberant
façade of polychromatic brickwork, turrets and small
windows masks a huge unsupported semi-cylindrical roof.
The arch, which spans 240 feet, was in the 1860s a
staggering piece of engineering by William H. Barlow.
Take a second look at the ticket office at the western end
of the station; it's all linen-fold oak panelling.

Tube: King's Cross, Euston

EXTRA . . . EXTRA . . . The area between King's Cross
and Euston, known as Somers Town, was once home for
the navvies who built the two stations. Later generations
of those same families still live in the area.

ST PAUL'S, Covent Garden, WC2

Known as 'The Actors' Church', St Paul's was designed
by Inigo Jones and completed in 1638. As you'll see from
the plaques both in the church and also in the pleasant
garden outside, many celebrities have been buried here,
including Claude Duval, the highwayman; Vivien Leigh,
the actress; and Dr Thomas Arne, who composed *Rule
Britannia*. The portico overlooking Covent Garden Piazza
was originally designed as the entrance, and it's here that
Eliza Doolittle meets Professor Higgins in Shaw's *Pyg-
malion*. However, this door is never used; you have to
use the entrances in the streets on the other three sides.

Tube: Leicester Square, Covent Garden
Open: Monday–Friday, 0900–1630

EXTRA . . . EXTRA . . . Also buried here is the satirist
Samuel Butler who left firm instructions that his feet
should touch one of the outer walls when he was interred.
Which wall? He didn't say! Why? He didn't explain!

ST PAUL'S CATHEDRAL, Ludgate Hill, EC4.
Tel: 01-248 4619/2705 (*see also Walk 5, page 255*)

St Paul's is the largest and most famous of the City
churches and its fame reached new heights in 1981 when
it was chosen for the Royal Wedding. Millions of television viewers saw Lady Diana Spencer arrive to pro-
nounce her marriage vows to the Prince of Wales. It
stands on the site of a medieval church which was
destroyed in the Great Fire of 1666. The present church,

designed by Wren, dates from 1675. The most outstanding feature of the building is the dome which is considered to be one of the finest in the world. Wander down the nave to the dome area and enjoy the sense of space as the Gothic plan combines gracefully with classical detail. (*See also National Service for Seafarers, page 226.*)

Tube: St Paul's
Open: daily

EXTRA . . . EXTRA . . . In the South Tower of St Paul's is 'Great Paul', the largest bell in England. Cast in Loughborough in 1882, it weighs 16¾ tons and is rung daily at 1300 for five minutes.

ST VEDAST-ALIAS-FOSTER, Foster Lane, EC2

A tranquil haven where silence on the part of the visitor comes naturally, this lovely simple church is a delight to visit. It was destroyed in the Great Fire of London, then rebuilt by Wren in 1670–3. Although badly damaged again in World War II, it has now been beautifully restored.

Tube: St Paul's
Open: Monday–Friday, 0600–1800, Saturday, 0700–0930, Sunday, 0700–1230

EXTRA . . . EXTRA . . . Vedast is the French equivalent of Foster, hence the rather long name for this lovely simple church.

SOUTHWARK CATHEDRAL, Cathedral Street, SE1. Tel: 01-407 2939

This beautiful cathedral is a peaceful haven nestling in a pretty garden; a tiny island flanked by river, bridge, railway and busy road. Successive early churches on the spot were destroyed by fire; their remains are about two feet below the present church level. On the north wall, door jambs of the Norman period can be glimpsed, along with a very old holy-water scoop. Take a look at the early 13th-century choir whose five bays are the oldest Gothic work in London. On a slab between the choir stalls, Edmund Shakespeare (*d.* 1607 and buried in an unmarked grave in the Cathedral) is commemorated, while in the South Aisle there is a memorial to his famous brother William. (*See also Church Music, page 18.*)

Tube: London Bridge
Open: daily 0900–1800

EXTRA . . . EXTRA . . . Much of the area around the cathedral is now derelict but worth wandering around as it still has lots of atmosphere. One of the streets which will inspire your imagination is Clink Street, SE1. Its name derives from a prison known as The Clink, now a colloquial word for prison but which probably originally came from an old French word *clique*, meaning a catch on the outside of a door.

THE TEMPLE, Fleet Street, EC4. Tel: 01-353 4355

The Temple, a quiet backwater off Fleet Street, was
originally the headquarters of the Order of Knights Templar of St John, founded in 1119 (*see also the Museum of
the Order of St John, page 123*). After the dissolution of
the Order in 1312 the ground was given to the Knights
Hospitallers who leased it to lawyers. When the Crown
took over the land in the early 17th century, lawyers were
given the freehold of the Inner and Middle Temple, and
it's now devoted entirely to the legal profession with
chambers (offices), lecture rooms and dining halls. However, the Knights Templar did leave their mark. The
Temple Church, which dates back to 1185, has on the
stone floor effigies of the Knights and their supporters.

There are two Inns of Court – the Inner Temple and
the Middle Temple. The hall of the Middle Temple is
open to the public. It was built in 1576 and although badly
damaged during World War II has been restored to its
previous grandeur with its ancient oak timbers, hammer-
beam roof and a serving table made from timbers of
Drake's *Golden Hind*. But the best thing about the
Temple is just to be able to walk through the maze of
alleyways and arches and breathe in the relaxed, tranquil
atmosphere.

Tube: Temple, Blackfriars
Open: Middle Temple Hall Monday–Friday, 1000–1200,
1500–1600. Closed in August
Temple Church daily, 1000–1600

EXTRA . . . EXTRA . . . Legend has it that it was in the
Inner Temple Gardens that the red and white roses were
first plucked at the beginning of the Wars of the Roses.
These roses are still grown here. You aren't allowed to

walk through the gardens, but there's nothing to stop you looking in through the railings.

TEMPLE OF MITHRAS, Queen Victoria Street, EC4

Excavations carried out in 1954 unearthed the remains of a Mithraic temple, built during the Roman occupation of London around A.D. 240. Mithras was a Persian god, popular with the Roman army. The temple was situated on the banks of the then sacred Walbrook stream which still runs under the City. Its reconstruction in Queen Victoria Street gives a clear idea of its original layout. Relics found nearby can be seen in the Museum of London, London Wall, EC2 (*see page 121*).

Tube: Mansion House, Bank

EXTRA . . . EXTRA . . . Nearby Watling Street, EC4, was part of a road system built by the Romans; the name is, however, Saxon.

TRAFALGAR SQUARE, WC2 (*see also Walk 4, page 253*)

This square, in the centre of London, is famed for its pigeons. But it's also of great historic interest. The square was dedicated to Lord Nelson in the 1820s and named after his great victory at the Battle of Trafalgar in 1805. Nelson's Column, the focal point of Trafalgar Square,

was designed by William Railton in 1840. The fluted
Corinthian column, which took three years to build,
stands 145 feet 6½ inches high and is crowned by a statue
of Nelson. Four magnificent bronze lions, designed by Sir
Edwin Landseer, guard the column at the base. (*See page
236 for details of the Christmas celebrations in the Square,
and also Trafalgar Day, page 228.*)

Tube: Charing Cross, Leicester Square
Open: all the time

EXTRA . . . EXTRA . . . Lord Nelson used to get his
cocked hats from James Lock, 6 St James's Street, SW1.
The shop, which is where the bowler hat originated, still
flourishes. Customers here still call a bowler hat a 'Coke'
after the man who first wore one.

TRINITY SQUARE GARDENS, EC3

These gardens, over-shadowed by the impressive façade
of Trinity House, have a dual interest. In the first place
they're a war memorial to the merchant seamen lost
fighting for their country; the hundreds of names recorded
all around the garden are a sombre reminder. Equally
sombre is the second reason for visiting these unusual
gardens. A small plaque, near the main road, marks the
site of the execution scaffold where 125 people from the
Tower of London were put to death. Names recorded
include: Thomas Cromwell, Earl of Essex (1540), Thomas
Wyatt (1554), Sir Thomas More (1535), Edward Planta-
genet (1521).

Tube: Tower Hill
Open: daily

EXTRA . . . EXTRA . . . When you get off the tube at
Tower Hill, look out for the modern statue of the Roman
Emperor Trajan in front of the city wall.

WESTMINSTER ABBEY, Parliament Square, SW1. Tel: 01-222 5152 (*see also Walk 4, page 251*)

The Abbey has, since 1066, been the setting for every
coronation. It contains the tombs of many kings and
queens, and memorials to many famous people. Elizabeth
I (*d*. 1603) is buried in the North Aisle of the Chapel of
Henry VII, while Elizabeth of York and Henry VII are
buried behind the altar. The whole chapel is ablaze with
the banners, crests and mantlings of the Knights of the
Order of the Bath. Colourful too is the memorial window
of the Royal Air Force Chapel which incorporates the
crests of the 68 Fighter Squadrons who took part in the
Battle of Britain in 1940. The architecture of the Abbey
is extremely impressive. Its focal point is the Sanctuary
and the High Altar which are surrounded by 13th-century
tombs and medieval wall-paintings. Nearby, Poet's
Corner includes memorials to Chaucer, Shakespeare,
Eliot, Auden and Dylan Thomas. The Abbey is huge, but
often extremely crowded – if you can, visit it out of the
normal tourist season.

Tube: St James's Park, Westminster
Open: Monday–Friday, 0900–1645, Saturday,
      0900–1445, 1545–1745

Important: The above times are for the whole Abbey. However, only a small portion is accessible without charge, except on a Wednesday evening (1800–1945) when the whole Abbey is open free of charge. (*See also Westminster Abbey Gardens, page 173; Florence Nightingale Commemoration Service, page 211; and Abbey Carol Services, page 234.*)

EXTRA . . . EXTRA . . . Parliament Square was laid out by Sir Charles Barry to complement his design for the Houses of Parliament (*page 184*). It contains a group of statues including Benjamin Disraeli, Abraham Lincoln, George Canning and Winston Churchill.

WESTMINSTER CATHEDRAL, Ashley Place, nr Victoria Street, SW1. Tel: 01-834 7452

Westminster Cathedral (not to be confused with Westminster Abbey) is both vast and imposing. Designed by John Bentley in an early-Christian Byzantine style, it has dramatic bands of red brick and Portland stone which are a sharp contrast to the tall, bland office blocks which surround it. The cathedral, 342 feet long, has the widest nave in England – 60 feet across. Down each side of the nave are small side-chapels usually only lit by twinkling candles. With such dim lighting the beauty of the mosaic ceilings can only be guessed, but occasionally figures and faces can be glimpsed among the shadows. A truly magnificent cathedral, off the usual tourist route, it is certainly worth a visit.

Tube: Victoria
Open: daily 0700–2000

EXTRA . . . EXTRA . . . The lift in the campanile is the third highest in any church, smaller only than those in the Riverside Church, New York.

CHAPTER THREE
Markets

BERWICK STREET AND RUPERT STREET,
W1

A stone's throw from Oxford Street and nestling between porn shops and strip shows these two streets of market stalls add colour and life to daytime Soho. It's worth spending a few hours here because, although the actual stalls are really only of interest to people wanting cheap, good-quality fruit and vegetables, the permanent shops nearby are fascinating. Camisa and Son (61 Old Compton Street, W1) sell the widest range of Italian cheeses and salamis you are likely to see anywhere, outside Italy that is!

Tube: Tottenham Court Road, Leicester Square, Oxford Circus
Open: Monday–Saturday, 0900–1700

EXTRA . . . EXTRA . . . Soho is noted for its cosmopolitan atmosphere. It became the chief foreign quarter of London when thousands of French Protestant refugees fled their country after the revocation of the Edict of Nantes in 1698.

BRICK LANE, Shoreditch, E1

Keep your eyes open for shifty characters doing a roaring trade in dodgy watches and jewellery – Brick Lane is not one of London's most honest markets! Stalls, barrows, makeshift shacks, sheds and pavement plots run from the railway bridge at Sclater Street to Bethnal Green Road with offshoots in side streets along the way. It's a real mixture of foodstuffs, clothes, records, bric-à-brac and hardware and although you need to be in the know to pick up any real bargains, it's certainly a lively place to visit. Nearby is another favourite Sunday market, Petticoat Lane (*see page 88*)

Tube: Liverpool Street
Open: Sunday 0800–1300

EXTRA . . . EXTRA . . . This is Jack the Ripper land. It was around these streets that Jack the Ripper committed five ghastly murders in the autumn of 1888. He always struck between midnight and 0600 on the first or last weekend of the month. His victims were prostitutes. Cashing in on this theme, there's a pub called Jack the Ripper in Commercial Street, E1, with photographs of the victims inside. On the wall outside the pub there's a list of all the murders giving times, places and names.

CAMDEN MARKETS

The walk between Chalk Farm and Camden Town tube stations is a real treat for bargain-hunters and antique enthusiasts, especially at weekends when there's almost a holiday atmosphere with stalls and shops spilling out onto the street selling all sorts of weird and wonderful wares. The main markets are:

CAMDEN ANTIQUES MARKET, corner of High Street and Buck Street, NW1
A pleasant if rather crowded group of stalls, this market is open four days a week. At the weekend the theme is clothes and fashion, Thursday is the day for antiques and bric-à-brac while on Friday the stalls sell arts and crafts.

Tube: Camden Town
Open: Thursday, 0700–1700, Friday–Sunday 0900–1700

CAMDEN CANAL MARKET, Chalk Farm Road, NW1
Warm and well-lit with piped music playing in the background, this covered market is reletively new with mod-cons including toilets and telephone. It opened in 1982 in the premises of Davy Autos, a panel-beating and spraying shop, and although rather overshadowed by Camden Lock opposite (*see below*) it has become as much-loved as all the Camden markets. There are plenty of handicrafts on sale, together with bric-à-brac and antiques and a mini bicycle mart. But as a rather refreshing change the sale of second-hand clothes is strictly forbidden.

Tube: Chalk Farm, Camden Town
Open: Saturday and Sunday, 0900–1800

CAMDEN LOCK, Dingwall's Wharf, NW1
Full of character and charm, Camden Lock, set in a disused timber wharf, is a thriving and extremely popular craft market. It seems that every available nook and cranny is filled with pottery, knitted garments, home-

baked cakes and all manner of crafts making it a colourful and exciting place to browse. The market has now grown to include an antiques section and a busy flea market in the Old Stables (once a horse hospital).

Tube: Camden Town, Chalk Farm
Open: Saturday and Sunday, 0900–1800

EXTRA . . . EXTRA . . . Another market in Camden, although quite different from the others, is Inverness Street. Selling fruit, vegetables and household goods, it is very much a market for the local people with a charm of its own. Open: Monday–Saturday, 0900–1700.

CAMDEN PASSAGE, Upper Street, Islington, N1

During the week this is a very civilized and sometimes expensive antique market with stalls selling a variety of antiques from prints and books to militaria. On Saturdays it is transformed into a lively flea market – popular with tourists and locals alike. The Mall, an indoor market with 38 galleries selling antiques, is open from Tuesdays to Saturdays, 1000–1700, with an early start on Wednesday when it's traders' day and the serious business is done.

Tube: Angel
Open: Wednesday, Saturday, 0800–1400, Thursday,
Friday, 0900–1700

EXTRA . . . EXTRA . . . Walk across to Islington Green, N1 – a triangular green with a statue of Sir Hugh

Myddelton in the centre. The old Collins' Music Hall
was at 10–11 Islington Green from 1862–1958. It was
founded by Sam Vagg, a chimney sweep who found
fame under his stage name, Sam Collins. Performers
here included Tommy Trinder, Charlie Chaplin and
Gracie Fields.

CHAPEL MARKET, Islington, N1

A friendly local market between Liverpool Street and
Penton Street selling all the usual goods. For the best
bargains go on Friday, Saturday and Sunday mornings.
The area is rather dirty and down at heel but the traders
all have friendly smiles on their faces and you'll be greeted
with lots of 'loves' and 'dearies'. If you're lucky you might
be able to shop to the sound of a busker.

Tube: Angel
Open: Tuesday, Wednesday, Friday and Saturday,
0800–1600, Sunday, 0800–1230

EXTRA ... EXTRA ... Charles Lamb, the famous
essayist, lived nearby at 64 Duncan Terrace, N1, from
1823 to 1827. At the time it was a red-light district. Lamb
lived here with his sister Mary.

COLUMBIA ROAD, Bethnal Green, E2

This is a real 'gardener's' market. It's one of the less well-known of the East End markets but is also one of the most attractive. With about 20 stalls selling pots, compost, tools and everything a gardener needs plus, of course, plenty of cut flowers and plants, it makes for a sweet-smelling and colourful visit.

Tube: Old Street, Liverpool Street, then bus 6, 35, 55
Open: Sunday, 0700–1330

EXTRA . . . EXTRA . . . You can admire the work of green-fingered experts with no compulsion to buy at one of London's nurseries or garden centres. Favourites are Rassell's (80 Earl's Court Road, W8); World's End Nurseries (441–57 King's Road, SW10); and Southwood's Village Nurseries (Townsend Yard, Highgate High Street, N6). Just don't be tempted to take any cuttings!

COVENT GARDEN, WC2

Much publicized shopping area and meeting place near to the Strand. When the old fruit and vegetable market moved to Nine Elms Lane in 1974 (*See page 189*) the area was given a total face-lift and it's now a place to spend a whole day. The Piazza, designed by Inigo Jones, is at the centre with specialist shops and many market stalls. Nearby, warehouses have been converted into offices, workshops, galleries and shops. All the specialist shops in and around the Piazza are worth browsing in – you'll find plenty of bizarre items as well as top-quality clothes and foodstuffs. Eating is expensive but there are plenty of places to perch so you can enjoy a packed lunch.

Tube: Covent Garden
Open: Shops Monday–Saturday, 0930–2000

EXTRA . . . EXTRA . . . Beware, the ghost of actor William Terris is said to haunt Covent Garden underground station! He was stabbed to death in 1897 by a jealous fellow actor at the nearby Adelphi Theatre.

EARL'S COURT EXHIBITION CENTRE MARKET, Earl's Court, SW6

You might have to pay to go into the many exhibitions held in the Earl's Court Exhibition Centre, but walk around to the car park at the back on a Sunday morning and you're free to enjoy the bustle of the weekly market. Stall-holders are usually in good voice shouting out their wares – and that's everything from second-hand clothes to cauliflowers. It's a favourite haunt for Earl's Court's student population searching for bargains.

Tube: Earl's Court, West Brompton
Open: Sunday, 0900–1400

EXTRA . . . EXTRA . . . Earl's Court gets its name from the courthouse of the Earls of Warwick and Holland who were once Lords of the Manor.

EAST STREET, Walworth, SE17

This large and bustling market runs along the entire length of East Street – and it's a long road! Trading gets off to a brisk start, particularly on Saturdays, as local people flood in to do their shopping. Stalls selling handbags, clothes, shoes and bric-à-brac are squeezed in beside barrows overflowing with fruit and vegetables. There are also a number of vendors offering traditional street market delicacies – cockles and mussels.

Tube: Elephant and Castle
Open: Tuesday–Saturday, 0830–1700, Sunday,
        0830–1300

EXTRA . . . EXTRA . . . East Street market was once frequented by a chirpy local youth – Charlie Chaplin.

ELECTRIC AVENUE, Brixton, SW9

Both the indoor and the outdoor markets here are worth a visit. There is a distinctly Caribbean flavour to the latter which sprawls around the Electric Avenue area selling mainly fruit and vegetables with the occasional hat stall, jewellery stand and second-hand clothes trader. The best day to go is Saturday when the area under the railway arches really comes to life – you may even pick up a bargain among the junk. The indoor market is more ordinary but there is still a good atmosphere.

Tube: Brixton
Open: Monday, Tuesday, Thursday and Saturday,
        0930–1730, Wednesday, 0900–1300

EXTRA . . . EXTRA . . . Grocers in the area sell some
very unusual foods – tinned ackee (a Jamaican delicacy),
egusi, kola nuts and soursubs, to name a few.

GREENWICH MARKETS, Greenwich, SE10

The two weekend markets here at Greenwich are becoming increasingly popular now that the whole area is
flourishing as a tourist spot. There are around 100 pitches
in the covered market in College Street selling antiques,
books, second-hand clothes, paintings, crafts and souvenirs. Smaller, but probably more interesting for just
browsing around, is the antiques market in the High
Road. There's an amazing selection of antiques and bric-
à-brac on sale making it a favourite haunt for collectors.

British Rail: Greenwich
Open: Covered market, Saturday and Sunday,
0900–1700; Antiques market, Saturday and
summer Sundays, 0800–1600

EXTRA . . . EXTRA . . . Greenwich was once a medieval
fishing village. Its name has a Saxon origin meaning 'green
village'. (*See also Greenwich Park, page 154.*)

JUBILEE MARKET, Covent Garden, WC2

This earthy market near Covent Garden Piazza (*see Covent Garden Market, page 80*), is a sort of continuation of the old Covent Garden fruit and vegetable market. The stalls change daily so the atmosphere depends on the day you choose for your visit. Mondays is the best day for the antiques buff or enthusiastic amateur; on Saturday it's devoted to crafts; Sundays is the day for the arts and crafts fair and the rest of the week it's mainly fruit and vegetables.

Tube: Covent Garden, Leicester Square
Open: Monday, 0600–1600, Tuesday to Friday, 0900–1600, Saturday and Sunday, 1000–1700

EXTRA ... EXTRA ... Theatre Royal, Drury Lane, WC2, is one of London's most famous theatres with a charter dating back to 1661. The actor David Garrick, who lived at 27 Southampton Street, WC2, was manager of the theatre in 1747–76 and as a tribute to his success as manager and actor Garrick Street, WC2, was named after him.

KENSINGTON MARKET, Kensington High Street, W8

This is *the* place to go if you want to know what all the trendiest people are wearing. You're not likely to pick up many bargains but from the choice of second-hand and designer clothes you'll pick up plenty of fashion tips. Look at the stall-holders too; their styles seem to change daily. Why not try on a few clothes yourself? There are changing cubicles and no obligation to buy.

Tube: High Street Kensington
Open: Monday–Saturday, 1000–1800

EXTRA . . . EXTRA . . . Kensington is named after the Kensige family who lived here in Saxon times. Incidentally, Kemsing, a village in Kent, is named after the same family. (*See also Kensington Gardens, page 160.*)

LEADENHALL MARKET, Gracechurch Street, EC3

Built in 1881, this typical Victorian covered market in the City teems with activity at lunchtime. Its impressive ironwork arcade, overshadowed by the equally impressive steel Lloyd's Building (*see page 185*), provides an atmospheric setting for fish, vegetables, flowers, meat, cheese and game stalls for which the market is today renowned.

Tube: Bank, Monument
Open: Monday–Friday, 0700–1600

EXTRA . . . EXTRA . . . In 1309 a mansion with a lead roof was built in this market area and nicknamed 'Leaden Hall'.

LEATHER LANE, EC1

A walk down Leather Lane (which stretches from Holborn to Clerkenwell Road) is a great way to spend a lunch hour. The stalls sell a huge variety of everyday things, especially household wares, clothes and general foods. But its name is misleading as there is no leather on sale here.

Tube: Chancery Lane
Open: Monday–Friday, 1000–1430

EXTRA . . . EXTRA . . . If you have time to spare take a five-minute walk down to Hatton Garden and let your imagination run riot as you window-shop in the medley of diamond and jewellery shops.

LOWER MARSH AND THE CUT, SE1

Lower Marsh was once the infamous meeting place for prostitutes in the days when costermongers' barrows lined its route. Today it is a busy lunchtime market which runs behind Waterloo Station. All the usual goods are on sale here, from second-hand clothes to fruit and vegetables. The lively atmosphere makes the market worth a visit.

Tube: Lambeth North, Waterloo
Open: Monday–Friday, 1000–1500

EXTRA . . . EXTRA . . . Don't miss the view from Waterloo Bridge at sunset. It was the inspiration for The Kinks' famous song 'Waterloo Sunset'.

NEW CALEDONIAN MARKET, Bermondsey
Square, Tower Bridge Road, SE1

By 0600 business is brisk here. It's an antiques dealers' market and the exchange of money is rapid. It's best seen before dawn when hundreds of torches flicker and flash in the darkness and the value of rings, goblets and watches is quickly decided.

Tube: London Bridge, Borough
Open: Friday, 0600–1200

EXTRA . . . EXTRA . . . Adjoining is the Church of St Mary Magdalene in Bermondsey Street, SE1. This church, founded in 1290 and rebuilt in 1680, is famed for its Gothic exterior. It stands on the site of the ancient Bermondsey Abbey.

NORTH END ROAD, Fulham, SW6

You'll find a wonderful range of fruits, flowers and vegetables in this large market that stretches along the east side of North End Road from Lillie Road to Vanston Place. The market was famous in the 1930s for its cheap foodstuffs with costermongers selling off their surplus goods at knock-down prices on Saturday evenings, and it's still a good place to find value for money.

Tube: Fulham Broadway, West Brompton
Open: Monday–Saturday, 0800–1800, Thursday, 0800–1300

EXTRA . . . EXTRA . . . A good time to visit Fulham is for the annual carnival in May. For more information about both the carnival and other features of interest in the borough contact: Hammersmith and Fulham Information Service, Town Hall, King Street, W6. Tel: 01-748 3020.

PETTICOAT LANE, Middlesex Street, E1

London's biggest market seems to spill over every side street and square in the area. It takes a whole morning to explore so get there early. The market runs through Middlesex Street and spreads into Cobb Street, Goulston Street, Toynbee Street and Wentworth Street among others. The stalls sell jumble, food, bric-à-brac – you name it, they sell it. You can always be sure of picking up a bargain.

The stalls in Cutler Street sell bargain jewellery but get there by 0730 and be prepared to do battle with the dealers. Totters Market, between Middlesex Street and Goulston Street, is where the rag and bone men, 'totters', take their junk. Again be there early, around 0600, which is when it's busiest.

These friendly markets will put a spring in your step and get your tastebuds tingling as you smell the delicious aromas of hot doughnuts and apple fritters. (*See also Brick Lane, page 76.*)

Tube: Liverpool Street, Aldgate, Aldgate East
Open: Petticoat Lane　Sunday, 0600–1330
　　　　Wentworth Street　Monday–Friday, 1030–1430,
　　　　Sunday, 0600–1230

Cutler Street   Sunday, 0700–1230
Totters Market   Sunday, 0600–1230

EXTRA . . . EXTRA . . . The street was known as Hog Lane in the 15th century, probably because pigs were kept in a field nearby. It was given the nickname Petticoat Lane in the 16th century when dealers in second-hand clothes began to set up stalls here.

PORTOBELLO ROAD, W10, W11

Crammed with junk, knick-knacks and the odd antique, Portobello Road is just the place to browse a few hours away – and maybe even pick up the odd bargain. Stalls in the street are great for poking around, but the shops along the side, although more expensive, are usually more exciting. It's at its best on Saturday when the antiques dealers set up stalls. There's a wonderful cosmopolitan atmosphere here. You'll see all ages, nationalities and hairstyles.

Tube: Ladbroke Grove, Notting Hill Gate
Open: Monday–Friday, 0800–1600 (Thursday, 0800–1300), Saturday, 0800–1800

EXTRA . . . EXTRA . . . The area, believe it or not, used to be farmland. The farm was called 'Porto Bello' to commemorate the capture of the town of Porto Bello on the Gulf of Mexico in 1739.

ROMAN ROAD, Bow, E3

Full of Cockney charm, this market, which stretches between St Stephen's Road and Parnell Road, is best known for its 'cabbages'. No, it's not another fruit and vegetable market, these 'cabbages' are actually clothes and fabrics, mostly discontinued lines, seconds and remnants. The quality is usually high and the prices so low that people come from near and far to barter for the bargains at 'The Roman'.

Tube: Bow Road, Mile End
Bus: 8, 8A, 52
Open: Tuesday and Thursday, 1000–1400, Saturday,
         0900–1730

EXTRA ... EXTRA ... Roman Road was originally known as Drift Way. It was renamed in the 19th century when it was found that it was probably built on or near the Roman road from London to Colchester.

SHEPHERD'S BUSH, W12

A large and very general market that stretches between Uxbridge Road and Goldhawk Road, alongside and under the railway viaduct. There is a strong Asian influence which shows in the bright colours of the boarding and the variety of goods for sale. If you want to get hold of any rare spices or Asian foods then this is the place to go. You could spend all day wandering around the stalls and factory shops. There are also plenty of cheap and good eating places in the market.

Tube: Shepherd's Bush, Goldhawk Road
Open: Monday–Saturday, 0930–1700, Thursday,
0930–1300

EXTRA . . . EXTRA . . . During World War I, the railway arches, which now shelter Shepherd's Bush Market, were used for billeting troops and stabling horses.

WALTHAMSTOW MARKET, High Street, E17

With more than a mile of stalls stretching along the High Street, this is reputed to be Britain's longest street market. Certainly there's plenty of variety, with around 500 stalls selling clothes, hardware and a fascinating selection of foodstuffs. You'll need to take your time to enjoy the variety and the friendly hustle and bustle of the market, and be warned, it's set on a fairly steep hill!

British Rail: Walthamstow Central, Walthamstow
Queens Road, St James Street
Open: Monday–Saturday, 0800–1800

EXTRA . . . EXTRA . . . The very first motor car in Britain was built in Walthamstow in 1894 by Frederick Bremer, a local engineer and plumber. And nearby Waltham Forest was the scene of the first succesful flight in a British aeroplane, a triplane built and designed by A. V. Roe in July 1909.

WEMBLEY MARKET, Wembley Stadium Car
Park, Wembley, Middlesex

There's a carnival atmosphere here every Sunday morning
with caravans selling colourful candy floss and toffee
apples standing side by side with stalls offering more
mundane wares – clothing, cheap jewellery and foodstuffs. With the huge Wembley stadium in the background, it's a well-positioned and lively Sunday morning
market.

Tube: Wembley Park
Open: Sunday, 0900–1400

EXTRA . . . EXTRA . . . Wembley stadium has played
host to many celebrated sporting events including the
1948 Olympic Games and 1966 World Cup.

WHITECHAPEL AND MILE END WASTE,
Whitechapel Road, E1

A long line of varied stalls running along the north side of
Whitechapel Road between Vallance Road and Brady
Street. Stall-holders shout out their wares which include
vegetables, books and jewellery. It's best on Friday and
Saturday when the market extends into Mile End Road
with stalls selling clothes and household goods.

Tube: Whitechapel
Open: Monday–Saturday, 0830–1700 (Thursday
        0830–1300)

EXTRA . . . EXTRA . . . Great men of Whitechapel
include Captain James Cook, who lived in Mile End Road

from 1764 to 1776; William Booth, who began his work with the Salvation Army in Mile End Waste in 1868; and Dr Barnardo, whose network of homes for children all over the country have saved many orphans. The first Dr Barnardo's Home was founded in 1870 near Ben Jonson Road, E1.

WOOLWICH MARKET, Beresford Square, SE18

Woolwich boasts two markets, one covered (and rather drab) and one outdoors. Make for the outdoor one; situated in a pedestrianized part of Woolwich it has become very popular with local people and is known as the place to pick up a bargain. There's certainly a variety of goods for sale: crockery, clothes, hardware, haberdashery, flowers, fruit and vegetables.

British Rail: Woolwich Arsenal
Open: Monday–Saturday, 0900–1700 (half day
       Thursday)

EXTRA . . . EXTRA . . . For a really unusual view of the river, including a glimpse of the distinctive hooded shapes of the Thames Barrier, take a trip across the water on the Woolwich Ferry. It's perhaps the only way to travel on the Thames for free!

CHAPTER FOUR

Museums, Collections and Galleries

BARNET MUSEUM, 31 Wood Street, Barnet,
Herts. Tel: 01-449 0321 ext. 4

The headquarters of the Barnet and District Local History
Society, this small but lively museum is packed with items
of interest to everyone. Old photographs, prints, books,
brass rubbings, samplers and household implements help
to make up the story of Barnet and the surrounding
district. Take special note of the relics of the Battle of
Barnet in 1471, one of the last of the Wars of the Roses
when the Earl of Warwick was killed.

Tube: High Barnet
Open: March–November, Tuesday–Thursday,
1430–1630, Saturday, 1000–1200, 1430–1630,
December–February, Tuesday–Thursday and
Saturday, 1400–1600

EXTRA . . . EXTRA . . . Walk along Wood Street in the
Arkley direction and you'll see Ravenscroft Gardens on
your right. These pleasant gardens are all that remains of
the great Barnet Common which used to be famous for
its highwaymen until it was enclosed in 1815.

Take the tube to Totteridge and as you come out of the
station you'll be faced with a glorious spread of green
grass and trees. It's an open invitation to walkers and
horse-riders.

BETHNAL GREEN MUSEUM OF CHILDHOOD, Cambridge Heath Road, E2.
Tel: 01-980 2415

Just the place to take the children for a day out or to relive a little of your own childhood. This museum, a branch of the Victoria and Albert Museum (*see page 136*), is a real Aladdin's Cave of toys, dolls and dolls' houses, teddy bears, games, puppets, nursery furniture and children's clothes dating back to the 18th century. Moving away from childhood, there's a collection of 19th- and 20th-century wedding-dresses and a display of some quite exquisite silk embroidery showing the history of the Spitalfields silk industry – once the main local industry. There are also many temporary exhibitions. You may need to go back several times to appreciate the full variety of items on display as it's rather like being a child in a sweet-shop – you don't know what to choose first!

Tube: Bethnal Green
Open: Mondays–Thursdays and Saturdays, 1000–1550
　　　　Sundays, 1430–1550

EXTRA . . . EXTRA . . . Keep your eyes open for statues of 'Charity Children' around London. Before State schools offered free education, charities used to set up special schools for poor children, and outside these schools were statues and carvings of the charity boys and girls. You'll see a good example outside Sir John Cass School, Aldgate, E1. She's dressed in a long black gown and carrying a Bible. (*See also Annual Events – Sir John Cass, Red Feather Day, page 202.*)

BRITISH MUSEUM, Great Russell Street, WC1.
Tel: 01-636 1555 (*see also Walk 2, page 243*)

One visit will just not be enough! Goodies housed here
include: the Rosetta Stone; Sutton Hoo Burial Ship;
mummies from Egypt; sculptures from Greece, and much,
much more. The British Museum Library is also well
worth visiting – there are over 10 million books occupying
110 miles of shelves. Beautiful collections of early printed
books, illuminated texts, and oriental manuscripts are of
particular interest. There are tours of the spectacularly
domed Reading Room which has its interior girders
picked out in gold leaf. Times of tours are shown just
inside the museum's main entrance.

Tube: Russell Square, Tottenham Court Road
Open: Museum, Monday–Saturday, 1000–1700, Sunday,
    1430–1800
    Library, Monday–Saturday, by tour only, on the
    hour, 1100–1600

EXTRA . . . EXTRA . . . The museum was founded in
1753 when King George II gave Royal assent to a bill in
the House of Lords which allowed the payment of
£20,000 for 'The Museum or Collection of Sir Hans
Sloane'.

THE BUILDING CENTRE, Store Street, WC1.
Tel: 01-637 1022

The Building Centre is to the building trade what the
Design Centre (*see page 105*) is to the design world – a
showcase. Here you can see topical exhibitions on a wide

range of themes from the many uses of brick to new architectural developments. There's also a permanent display of building products, a bookshop and an information exchange with an index of over 80,000 trade names. But even if you're not in the trade, you're both free and welcome to browse through the centre; you'll undoubtedly learn something about the industry.

Tube: Goodge Street, Tottenham Court Road
Open: Monday–Friday, 0930–1700, Saturday, 1000–1300

EXTRA . . . EXTRA . . . Nearby Bedford Square is an excellent example of urban Georgian architecture; its elegant façades are almost totally intact. But take a careful look at the doorways, they're made from Coade stone (*see Royal Festival Hall, page 28*). Along with the capitals and the mouldings, the doorways are from stock patterns. So, for all its completeness and despite showing a close resemblance to the work of James Adam, Bedford Square's design is not attributed to a particular architect; it is, in fact, an example of developer construction.

CHARTERED INSURANCE INSTITUTE MUSEUM, 20 Aldermanbury, EC2. Tel: 01-606 3835

This museum is all about fire and fire fighting and although it is tiny every corner is crammed full with interest. In pride of place are three old fire engines, one of which is still in working order and used for celebrations, but there's also a whole array of fire-fighting tools, fire buckets, helmets, medals and old documents. As you walk up the stairs to the museum, don't miss the Institute's fine collection of British and foreign fire-marks and fire-plates which line the walls. It's impressively large and varied with fire-marks dating back to 1682.

Tube: St Paul's, Bank, Mansion House, Moorgate
Open: by appointment only, Monday–Friday, 1000–1600

EXTRA . . . EXTRA . . . Fire-marks were first introduced after the Great Fire of London. House-owners realized it was necessary to insure their homes against risk of fire and insurance companies each employed fire brigades to protect the property of their policy-holders. Fire-marks were attached to the exterior of the buildings to identify which insurance company covered the premises. No fire brigade would put out a fire unless they could see their plaque, they'd just leave it to blaze away. Eventually, the brigades agreed to co-operate and the London Fire Engine Establishment was formed in 1833. However, you can still see fire-marks on some buildings in London.

CHURCH FARM HOUSE MUSEUM, Greyhound Hill, Hendon, NW4. Tel: 01-203 0130

This fascinating museum is set up in an old farmhouse, possibly the oldest surviving dwelling-place in North London, and describes domestic life in the 17th–19th centuries. Look especially for the kitchen where you can almost smell baking bread. There are also many temporary special exhibitions staged at the museum, concentrating mainly on local history and the decorative arts.

Tube: Hendon Central
Open: Monday–Saturday, 1000–1300, 1400–1730,
(Tuesday 1000–1300 only), Sunday, 1400–1730

EXTRA . . . EXTRA . . . Behind the museum is Sunny Hill Park which is mainly laid to grass and is a pleasant place for a walk. There are also tennis courts and a playground area.

CLOCKMAKERS' COMPANY MUSEUM,
Guildhall Library, Aldermanbury, EC2.
Tel: 01-606 3030 ext. 2866 (*see also Walk 5, page 257*)

This collection of antique clocks and watches of the Worshipful Company of Clockmakers makes you realize just how much we take our digital watches and alarm clocks for granted. All exhibits are fascinating, but make a special note to see the display charting the progress of the wrist-watch between 1580 and 1884. (*See also Guildhall, page 42*).

Tube: Bank, Moorgate, St Paul's
Open: Monday–Friday, 0930–1645

EXTRA . . . EXTRA . . . The clock outside Carter's, the gentlemen's outfitters in Old Kent Road, SE1, is headed by the bust of a bowler-hatted gentleman. The hat is raised at midday.

THE COMMONWEALTH INSTITUTE,
230 Kensington High Street, W8. Tel: 01-603 4535

There's so much to see at this museum and arts centre that it's hard to fit it all into one day. The exhibition is on three floors, with each Commonwealth country mounting an individual collection of posters, charts, statues, costumes and films to give as clear a picture as possible of their environment and an insight into how the people work, live, eat and dress. There are also special exhibitions and a library and information centre. The staff here show great concern for disabled people.

Tube: High Street Kensington
Open: Monday–Saturday, 1000–1730
Sunday, 1400–1730

EXTRA . . . EXTRA . . . The materials for the Commonwealth Institute were given by different Commonwealth countries. The copper for the roof (25 tons) was donated by Zambia.

THE CRAFTS COUNCIL GALLERY,
12 Waterloo Place, SW1. Tel: 01-930 4811

This is the national centre of The Crafts Council, set up to promote fine craftsmanship, so you can always expect the work on show in their gallery to be of a high standard. The exhibitions, many of which are free, change regularly and cover both contemporary and historic crafts, from home and abroad. There's also a library and information centre here. You'll find everyone extremely helpful and more than ready to answer your questions and point you in the direction of other galleries worth visiting.

Tube: Piccadilly Circus, Charing Cross
Open: Tuesday–Saturday, 1000–1700, Sunday, 1400–1700

EXTRA . . . EXTRA . . . Orange Street, WC2, off Haymarket, is just a short walk away. On the south side of the street at the Haymarket end you'll see a stone plaque saying 'James Street 1673'. The street has since been renamed, but as this is one of the oldest street name signs in London it's still on show.

CROSBY HALL, Cheyne Walk, SW3.
Tel: 01-352 9663

This medieval hall was originally built in 1466 as part of Crosby Place, Bishopsgate, for Sir John Crosby, a wealthy wool merchant. It was later the home of the Duke of Gloucester (later Richard III) and Sir Thomas More, among others. The hall survived the Great Fire and in 1908–10 was moved stone by stone to its present site – a sort of home from home as it used to be the garden of Sir Thomas More's Chelsea house.

Tube: Sloane Square, then 137 bus
Open: by appointment only; for opening times telephone above number

---

EXTRA . . . EXTRA . . . The landscape painter, J. M. W. Turner, lived and worked at 119 Cheyne Walk.

Turner loved his cottage because of the splendid view it afforded of the Thames. Apparently he said to one visitor, 'There you see my study – sky and water. Are they not glorious? Here I have my lessons day and night.'

DESIGN CENTRE, 28 Haymarket, SW1.
Tel: 01-839 8000

Articles here are chosen by the Council of Industrial Design as representative of the best in modern British craftsmanship. The displays change regularly to keep up with ideas and trends. There is also an enquiry service which will help you obtain information on any product, and a collection of samples of textiles, ceramics and floor-coverings.

Tube: Piccadilly Circus
Open: Monday and Tuesday, 1000–1800,
Wednesday–Saturday, 1000–2000, Sunday,
1300–1800

EXTRA . . . EXTRA . . . Haymarket was once the centre of a market selling hay – it's very hard to imagine today, but from its establishment early in Elizabeth I's reign until 1830 the market thrived.

GEFFRYE MUSEUM, Kingsland Road, Shoreditch, E2. Tel: 01-739 8368

Take a look at how a typical middle-class family would have furnished a home from 1600 to 1939. With tremendous attention to detail, many period settings have been created with panelling, furniture and domestic equipment. There's also an open-hearth kitchen and 18th-century woodworker's shop on show. The museum was originally the almshouses of the Ironmongers' Company, built in 1713 with funds bequeathed by Sir Robert Geffrye, Lord Mayor of London in 1685. The almshouses' original Chapel, with a rare four-tiered pulpit, still stands. Don't be afraid to ask the attendants for information; they're some of the friendliest in London.

Tube: Liverpool Street, Old Street
Open: Tuesday–Saturday, 1000–1700, Sunday,
　　　　1400–1700

EXTRA . . . EXTRA . . . Rest awhile in the gardens at the front of the museum. Hidden from the busy Kingsland Road by London plane trees, it's an ideal retreat for some quiet reading or thinking.

GEOLOGICAL MUSEUM, Exhibition Road, South Kensington, SW7. Tel: 01-589 3444

Diamonds, opals, jade, amethyst, garnet – these are just a few of the precious and semi-precious stones on display both in their raw, natural state and in the more recognizable cut and polished form. This display of *Gemstones* is one of the permanent exhibitions, which also include *Story of the Earth*, *Britain Before Man*, and *British Fossils*. And of special interest is a piece of Moon-rock, the only sample on public view in Britain, which was brought back from the Apollo 16 mission. There are regular free lectures and films on all aspects of geology and mineralogy.

Tube: South Kensington
Open: free only Monday–Friday, 1630–1800, Saturday
and Sunday, 1700–1800

EXTRA . . . EXTRA . . . Exhibition Road was named after The Great Exhibition of 1851, in Hyde Park, had proved to be such a success.

GRANGE MUSEUM, Neasden Lane, NW10.
Tel: 01-452 8311

Situated slap bang in the middle of busy Neasden round-about, the Grange Museum looks a rather strange and lonely sight. But once inside (you have to cross a pedestrian bridge to get there!) you're transported back in time. The museum has displays showing the history of local people in the suburbs of Wembley and Willesden, including a special section devoted to the British Empire Exhibition at Wembley in 1924 and '25. The staff are friendly and well-informed and although it is rather a trek to get to the museum, it is worth it. Special exhibitions are held from time to time.

Tube: Neasden
Open: Monday–Friday, 1200–1700 (2000 Wednesday),
          Saturday, 1000–1700

EXTRA . . . EXTRA . . . It might sound like a crazy idea
to picnic in the middle of a roundabout but the gardens
surrounding the museum are sheltered and visitors are
welcome. Look out for the old well.

GUILDHALL LIBRARY, Aldermanbury, EC2.
Tel: 01-606 3030 (*see also Walk 5, page 255*)

In the West Wing of Guildhall, this collection of reference
material, including manuscripts, books, maps and prints,
illustrates the history and development of London. It is
so comprehensive that people come from all over the
world to use the library. The atmosphere is remarkably
informal, and although you can't take any of the books
away, everyone is welcome to browse and read. There is
also an exhibition room of famous books and manuscripts.

Tube: Bank, Moorgate, St Paul's
Open: Monday–Saturday, 0930–1700

EXTRA . . . EXTRA . . . To the west of Guildhall is
Aldermanbury which is named after a 'bury' or court of
an Alderman.

GUNNERSBURY PARK MUSEUM, Gunnersbury Park, Pope's Lane, W5. Tel: 01-992 1612

Head first for the impressive transport collection. Here you can see the coaches belonging to the Rothschild family. There's also a tandem tricycle, a manually operated fire-engine and a bath chair similar to that which Baroness de Rothschild would have used. As well as this collection of transport there are local archaeological finds, displays of costumes, toys and dolls, all covering the history of the London boroughs of Ealing and Hounslow. The museum is housed in the ornate rooms of the former Rothschild country residence.

Tube: Acton Town
Open: March–October: Monday–Friday,1300–1700
weekends, 1400–1800
November–February: Monday–Friday, 0900–1600
weekends, 1400–1600

EXTRA . . . EXTRA . . . You can spend an hour or so wandering through the grounds, Gunnersbury Park, which houses other historic buildings. It's always a hive of sporting activity on Saturday afternoons and Sunday mornings. Kensington Cemetery adjoins the park and contains the Katyn Memorial, erected in 1976 to commemorate Polish officers massacred in World War II.

HARROW MUSEUM AND HERITAGE CENTRE,
The Tithe Barn, Headstone Manor Recreation Ground, Headstone Lane, Pinner, Middlesex. Tel: 01-861 2626

Harrow is perhaps best known for its public school (*see Old Speech Room Gallery, page 128*), but recently there's been a big promotion drive to make people aware of all the other features in the borough. And with a history dating back to pre-Roman times, some beautiful Green Belt parks with way-marked walks, and the charming village-like atmosphere of areas such as Kenton, Stanmore and Pinner (which still holds an annual fair dating back to the 14th century), there's certainly plenty to see and do here. A good starting point to find out more about Harrow and its eventful past is this 'living museum' housed in a tithe barn. Opened in 1986, it's a lively exhibition space with changing displays on the area, pottery and craft demonstrations, and summer entertainments.

British Rail: Headstone Lane
Open: Tuesday–Friday, 1230–1600, weekends, 1030–1700

EXTRA . . . EXTRA . . . Other attractions in Harrow include the ancient church of St Mary's, which stands on the hill, and Grim's Dyke, home of the librettist W. S. Gilbert until 1911, now a luxury hotel. For full details of the area contact Harrow Information Centre, Civic Centre, Station Road, Harrow, Middlesex. Tel: 01-863 5611 ext. 2102/3. Open: Monday–Friday, 0830–1700.

HEINZ GALLERY, 21 Portman Square, W1.
Tel: 01-580 5533

This tiny gallery (just one small room) off Oxford Street is worth dropping into if you're in the area. It belongs to the Royal Institute of British Architects and its regularly changing exhibitions (about six a year) are all associated with architecture. However, you don't have to be an expert to enjoy buildings and there's often a helpful explanatory leaflet provided; do take a look.

Tube: Marble Arch
Open: Monday–Friday,1100–1700, Saturday, 1000–1300
(the gallery is closed throughout the whole of August and between exhibitions)

EXTRA . . . EXTRA . . . The Royal Institute of British Architects also has an extensive collection of drawings covering all countries and periods which you can see for free by making an appointment – telephone 01-580 5533 for details.

HOGARTH'S HOUSE, Hogarth Lane, Great West Road, Chiswick, W4. Tel: 01-994 6757

William Hogarth, artist and satirist, famed for his moral paintings of the 18th century, including 'Gin Lane' and 'The Rake's Progress', used this simple house as his country retreat from 1749 to 1764. And although it is now surrounded by office blocks and fronted by a busy road, once you're inside it is easy to recapture the peace and tranquillity enjoyed by Hogarth in his 'country box by the Thames'. There's some period furniture and memorabilia on display but the house is essentially a showcase for Hogarth's paintings and engravings. It's not a place for a whistle-stop visit – you'll want to soak up the homely atmosphere, linger over Hogarth's works, taking in all the detail and moral significance, and perhaps spend a while in the beautiful little garden. Notice the mulberry tree which still bears enough fruit to make mulberry tarts, Hogarth's traditional gift to foundling children in Chiswick. The curator is extremely knowledgeable and will happily give you an enlightening tour of the house and paintings if you ask.

Tube: Turnham Green
Open: April–September, Monday and
           Wednesday–Saturday, 1100–1800, Sunday,
           1400–1800; October–March, Monday and
           Wednesday–Saturday 1100–1600, Sunday,
           1400–1600. Closed first two weeks in September
           and last three weeks in December.

EXTRA . . . EXTRA . . . Hogarth died here in 1764. He was buried with his wife, Jane, and sister, Anne, and you can see the tomb in Chiswick churchyard, a peaceful spot on the banks of the River Thames, just a short walk away.

HORNIMAN MUSEUM, 100 London Road, Forest Hill, SE23. Tel: 01-699 2339

Man and his environment is the theme for the collections and displays housed in this original Art Nouveau-style building. The exhibits cover anthropology, ethnology and natural history. There's also a fascinating collection of musical instruments from all over the world. It was founded in the 1890s by Frederick J. Horniman, the much travelled head of the family tea firm, who decided to open his private collection of souvenirs to the public. The museum has become a centre for education with free lectures, concerts, courses and horticultural demonstrations for adults and children. The tearooms are open in the afternoon.

Bus: 12, 12A, 63, 176, 185, 194, P4; (Sunday only) 12B, 194A
British Rail: Forest Hill
Open: Monday–Saturday, 1030–1800, Sunday, 1400–1800

EXTRA . . . EXTRA . . . Enjoy a nature trail around the Horniman Gardens or along the disused railway line running from London Road to Langton Rise. For details ask at the museum reception.

IMPERIAL WAR MUSEUM, Lambeth Road, SE1.
Tel: 01-735 8922

Fifteen-inch naval guns in the forecourt welcome you to this museum which is top of the list of favourites for anyone interested in war. With guns, tanks, medals, aircraft and armoured fighting vehicles, this collection outlines the activities of the two World Wars and all the other major conflicts involving Britain and the Commonwealth since 1914. They also stage special exhibitions and regular film shows.

Tube: Lambeth North, Elephant and Castle
Open: Monday–Saturday, 1000–1750, Sunday,
           1400–1730

EXTRA . . . EXTRA . . . Just a few minutes away is Lambeth Walk. It's now a rather grim pedestrian shopping precinct with a few market stalls on Friday and Saturday, but it used to be a thriving market, the centre of community life and entertainment. Indeed, it was so popular that it was immortalized in that famous song of 1937: 'Any time you're Lambeth way, any evening, any day, you'll find us all doin' the Lambeth Walk.'

JEWISH MUSEUM, Woburn House, Upper Woburn Place, WC1. Tel: 01-387 3081

A tiny but exquisite collection of Jewish antiquities. Don't be put off by the long trek necessary to find the museum in Woburn House, a Jewish community centre – it's well worth the effort.

Tube: Euston
Open: Monday–Thursday, 1230–1500, Sunday,
           1030–1245

EXTRA . . . EXTRA . . . Do take a few minutes to look at picturesque Woburn Walk, WC1 – a small, car-free lane lined by early 19th-century houses with pretty shopfronts. W. B. Yeats lived at number 5.

KEATS HOUSE, Wentworth Place, Keats Grove, Hampstead, NW3. Tel: 01-435 2062

This is where John Keats, the poet, lived for two years, and where he became engaged to Fanny Brawne, who lived next door. The white Regency house is now an excellent museum devoted to his life and works. Guided tours can be arranged – telephone for details.

Tube: Hampstead, Belsize Park
Open: Monday–Saturday, 1000–1300, 1400–1800,
         Sunday, 1400–1700

EXTRA . . . EXTRA . . . The plum tree in the garden was planted to replace the one under which Keats wrote *Ode to a Nightingale.* However, the mulberry tree on the front lawn probably dates back to Stuart times.

KENWOOD (The Iveagh Bequest), Hampstead Lane, NW3. Tel: 01-348 1286 (*see also Walk 6, page 257*)

This impressive building is set in characteristically 18th-century landscaped parkland. It's the home of a fine collection of paintings, including a self-portrait by Rembrandt. Other features include one of the finest Adam rooms in existence – the Adam Library. Refreshments are available in the Coach House and Old Kitchen Restaurant, and you're free to wander around the grounds which adjoin Hampstead Heath (*see page 156*). Look out for Dr Johnson's summer house tucked away behind trees.

Tube: Golders Green or Archway, then bus 210
Open: April–September, daily, 1000–1900;

October, February and March, daily, 1000–1700;
November and January, daily, 1000–1600

EXTRA . . . EXTRA . . . The 17th-century Spaniards
Inn, also in Hampstead Lane, has so many literary and
historic connections and so many interesting things on
display that it could almost be a museum itself. It's
mentioned in the fictional tale of Dick Turpin's ride to
York, and it's the setting for Mrs Bardell's tea party in
Dickens's *Pickwick Papers*. Among its regulars have been
Keats, Byron and Shelley.

KINGSTON-UPON-THAMES MUSEUM AND HERITAGE CENTRE, Fairfield West, Kingston-upon-Thames, Surrey. Tel: 01-546 5386

From the outside, it appears to be simply a tourist
information centre but step a bit further inside and you'll
find not only maps and leaflets about local attractions but
a local history museum too. It's also the home of a rare
collection portraying the work of one of Kingston's most
notable sons, Edward Muybridge (1830–1904), the
pioneer of cinematography. Don't miss his zoopraxiscope
– an amazing magic lantern contraption first used in 1879
to show moving picture sequences.

British Rail: Kingston
Tube: Richmond, then bus 65 or 71
Open: Monday–Saturday, 1000–1700

EXTRA . . . EXTRA . . . While you're in Kingston-upon-
Thames, visit the Coronation Stone beside Guildhall in

the centre of the town. This slab of grey sandstone is where seven Anglo-Saxon kings were crowned.

LEIGHTON HOUSE MUSEUM AND ART GALLERY, 12 Holland Park Road, Kensington, W14. Tel: 01-602 3316

This was the home of Victorian artist Frederic Lord Leighton, President of the Royal Academy until he died in 1896. He designed the house and studio with George Aitchison. Take special note of the Arab Room, with its fountain and dome, which houses Leighton's collection of tiles from different countries. Leighton House contains a permanent exhibition of Victorian art by Leighton and his friends. There are also frequent special exhibitions here.

Tube: High Street Kensington, Holland Park
Open: Monday–Saturday, 1100–1700 (1800 weekdays during special exhibitions)

EXTRA . . . EXTRA . . . Next door at 14 Holland Park Road is a house built at the same time as Leighton House (1864–6), but with a different and rather chaotic design. This was the work of Philip Webb, who designed the house for Valentine Prinsep, an artist.

LIVESEY MUSEUM, 682 Old Kent Road, SE15.
Tel: 01-639 5604

This small, friendly south London museum has successive changing exhibitions. It is aimed mainly at the local community, and many of the exhibitions deal with the history of Southwark. There are often free work sheets for children, and the museum staff are very helpful. Exhibitions have included: *The History of Craft*, *The River Thames*, *Music Halls*, and *Evolution* – so it's best to give them a ring to find out what's on.

Tube: Elephant and Castle, then bus 21, 53, 78, 141, 177
Open: Monday–Saturday,1000–1700 (during exhibitions)

EXTRA ... EXTRA ... Why not visit another small South London collection? The Cuming Museum, 155–7 Walworth Road, SE17, tel: 01-703 3324/5529, has a permanent exhibition devoted to Southwark's history. Look out for the mechanical cow!

Tube: Elephant and Castle
Open: Monday–Friday, 1000–1730 (Thursday until 1900), Saturday, 1000–1700

LONDON TAXI MUSEUM, 1–3 Brixton Road, SW9. Tel: 01-735 7777

You can't be in London for more than a few minutes before you see a black London taxi-cab; then another and another and another. There are an estimated 30,000 black taxis in the London area. In the small, very much off-the-beaten-track Taxi Museum you can see just how they developed their present distinctive shape. However, this is a museum for real enthusiasts – there are very few labels to help the less knowledgeable – but you can ask for a free information sheet from the office. The earliest taxi you'll see dates from 1907; in order to comply with the regulations of the day it has no front brakes! The first taxi to be fitted with front brakes was the Beardmore (manufactured 1929–35). You can see the only one still in existence, along with the first cab to have an illuminated roof sign – the Austin LL (1938). You can also see a totally unique taxi – the Lucas Electric (1975–6) which is powered by a rechargeable battery – and it isn't black!

Tube: Oval
Open: Monday–Friday, 0900–1700, Saturday, 0900–1200

EXTRA ... EXTRA ... Nearby is the famous Oval Cricket Ground.

MARX MEMORIAL LIBRARY, 37a Clerkenwell Green, EC1. Tel: 01-253 1485

It's easy to walk straight past 37a Clerkenwell Green, as there's little to publicize what lies behind the door. However, this house, which has had such strong links with socialist and radical organizations through the years, is now home to the Marx Memorial Library. Founded in 1933 to mark the 50th anniversary of Marx's death, it has built up a unique collection of over 100,000 books, pamphlets and periodicals, as well as badges, coins and medals all connected with Marxism and the broad labour movement. It's rather cramped inside, but the staff are more than happy to show you around – do ask to see some of the library's prized exhibits, including a copy of Volume One of Marx's *Capital* signed by Engels, and the plate commemorating the Paris Commune of 1871. The room where Lenin edited his newspaper *Iskra* (The Spark) in 1902–3 is also on view. To study and borrow the library's books, you have to be a member, but everyone is welcome to browse and to attend the regular free lectures and occasional exhibitions.

Tube: Farringdon
Open: Monday and Friday, 1400–1800,
Tuesday–Thursday, 1400–2100, Saturday
1100–1300

EXTRA ... EXTRA ... Clerkenwell has had radical associations since the Peasants' Revolt of 1381; the Green itself was once a well-established speaking place. It was here that William Cobbett addressed a meeting in 1826 against the Corn Laws, and in 1838 a large gathering paid tribute to the first of the Tolpuddle Martyrs on his return from transportation.

MUSEUM OF GARDEN HISTORY, St Mary-at-Lambeth, next Lambeth Palace, Lambeth Palace Road, SE1. Tel: 01-373 4030

The historic church of St Mary-at-Lambeth at the gates of Lambeth Palace was saved from demolition in the 1970s by the determined efforts of The Tradescant Trust. It is now a museum with permanent and temporary exhibitions covering everything of interest to gardeners and garden historians. The Tradescant Exhibition, tracing the lives and work of the two John Tradescants, father and son, famous Royal gardeners and collectors of 'all things strange and rare', is most fascinating. It's these two men whom we can thank for discovering and importing many of our favourite garden plants and flowers. They are buried in the churchyard, which has now been opened as a period garden with 17th-century plants and called The Tradescant Garden in their honour.

Tube: Waterloo, then bus 507, Lambeth North
Open: Monday–Friday, 1100–1500, Sunday, 1030–1700,
(Closed second Sunday in December–second
Sunday in March)

EXTRA . . . EXTRA . . . Also buried in the churchyard is Captain William Bligh (1754–1817) who is best known for his ship *Bounty* and its famous mutiny. Captain Bligh lived at 3 Durham Place, now 100 Lambeth Road, SE1.

MUSEUM OF LONDON, 150 London Wall, EC2.
Tel: 01-600 3699 (*see also Walk 5, page 255*)

A really excellent museum which doesn't reduce the visitor to an exhausted wreck after half an hour. The careful and unusual layout of the galleries keeps the exhibits alive while providing a detailed history. Prehistory, Medieval, Tudor, Stuart, Georgian, Victorian and 20th century changes to the capital are all recorded. History has been encapsulated by careful selection and presentation: a Woolworth counter top given as much

attention as a Lord Mayor's coach. The effect is sometimes that of a peep-show offering an opportunity to
glimpse inside an air-raid shelter, a working-class kitchen
or a Victorian shop. Look out for the Fire of London
Experience (it would spoil the fun to tell you what it is,
but children love it!).

Tube: St Paul's, Moorgate, Barbican (closed Sundays)
Open: Tuesday–Saturday, 1000–1750, Sunday,
          1400–1750

EXTRA . . . EXTRA . . . The cafeteria at the Museum of
London is adequate if you want to stay indoors but if you
have a packed lunch make for the Postman's Park in
Little Britain, EC1. These pretty gardens were opened in
1880 and contain a memorial arcade of plaques, many
designed by G. F. Watts, which touchingly record the
heroic deeds of ordinary people. There are plenty of
benches too, making this an ideal refuge in the concrete
jungle of the City.

MUSEUM OF MANKIND, 6 Burlington Gardens,
W1. Tel: 01-437 2224 (*see also Walk 1, page 241*)

Although a specialized section of the British Museum,
this museum isn't only for anthropologists. Filled with
examples of the day-to-day paraphernalia of non-Western
peoples it provides a fascinating insight into the lifestyles
of other societies. It's perhaps more interesting than many
other museums because in many instances it records living
history rather than past civilizations. Particular effort is

always made with the temporary exhibitions. They also organize film shows and have a large reference library.

Tube: Green Park, Piccadilly Circus
Open: Monday–Saturday, 1000–1700, Sunday,
        1430–1800

EXTRA . . . EXTRA . . . Nearby is Burlington Arcade, W1, a covered row of rather superior shops selling, among other luxuries, cashmere scarves, pipes, jade and jewellery. It was built in 1819 and still retains the style of the period. Lovely to walk through. And have a chuckle to yourself as you think back to the mid-19th century – at that time it was a popular haunt for prostitutes who would invite their customers into furnished rooms above the shops. Incidentally, you are forbidden to run, sing or whistle here – a uniformed beadle will rush up and stop you, should you dare!

MUSEUM OF THE ORDER OF ST JOHN, St
John's Gate, St John's Lane, Clerkenwell, EC1.
Tel: 01-253 6644 ext. 35

The museum is small but fascinating. It includes old books dating from 1425, armour, paintings, and historical objects relating to the Order. There is also an interesting exhibition of Clerkenwell's history and a museum devoted to the St John's Ambulance Brigade which was launched from St John's Gate in 1837. (*See also Temple, page 67, and Order of St John, page 52.*)

Tube: Farringdon, Barbican
Open: Tuesday and Friday, 1000–1800, Saturday,
      1000–1600

EXTRA . . . EXTRA . . . A pilgrimage of the Worshipful
Company of Parish Clerks used to visit Clerkenwell Green
to perform mystery plays telling the story of the Bible in
dramatic form.

NATIONAL ARMY MUSEUM, Royal Hospital
Road, Chelsea, SW3. Tel: 01-730 0717

Opened by the Queen in 1971, this museum gives a
detailed picture of the history of the British Army during
the five centuries of its existence. With the permanent
exhibition, *From Flanders to the Falklands*, opened in
June 1983, it now gives the whole story. There are
collections of paintings, weapons, uniforms and personal
mementoes – all displayed with clear captions along an
easy-to-follow route. Special exhibits are the skeleton of
'Marengo', Napoleon's favourite charger, and Florence
Nightingale's lamp.

Tube: Sloane Square
Open: Monday–Saturday, 1000–1730, Sunday,
      1400–1730

EXTRA . . . EXTRA . . . Nearby at 23 Tedworth Square,
SW3, Mark Twain lived from 1896 to 1897. It was here
that he wrote *Following the Equator* – a record of a world
trip which included his visit to London. Mark Twain is

probably best remembered for his books *The Adventures of Tom Sawyer* and *The Adventures of Huckleberry Finn*.

NATIONAL GALLERY, Trafalgar Square, WC2.
Tel: 01-839 3321

The National Gallery has a huge collection of art with examples of Western European schools from around 1300 to about 1900. A particularly interesting section is room 46 which displays the large painting *Water Lilies* by Monet, with thoughtfully provided seating. Look out too for masterpieces by Uccello, Titian, Tintoretto, Rembrandt, Rubens, Poussin, Turner, Watteau, Canaletto, Goya, Leonardo da Vinci and many more. There are free lunch-time lectures (*see pages 22–23*) and children's quizzes throughout the year. The coffee rooms are pleasantly decorated and, apart from a rushed lunch period, offer a tranquil place for tired feet to regenerate; they are reasonably priced and offer a good selection.

Tube: Charing Cross, Leicester Square
Open: Monday–Saturday, 1000–1800, Sunday,
1400–1800

EXTRA . . . EXTRA . . . Stand on the steps of the National Gallery for a spectacular view of Trafalgar Square (*page 68*) with Whitehall stretching majestically into the distance. You get a great feeling of being in the heart of London.

NATIONAL MUSEUM OF LABOUR HISTORY, Limehouse Town Hall, Commercial Road, E14. Tel: 01-515 3229

Whatever your politics, this small museum, which exhibits photographs, medallions, desks, pamphlets and other memorabilia of Labour history, is a fascinating place to browse. Well displayed items relate to events studied at school – Tolpuddle Martyrs, General Strike, Suffragettes.

Tube: Aldgate East, then bus 5, 15, 23, 40
Open: Tuesday–Saturday, 0930–1700, Sunday,
1430–1730

EXTRA . . . EXTRA . . . In the churchyard next door to Limehouse Town Hall is a pyramid!

NATIONAL PORTRAIT GALLERY, 2 St Martin's Place, WC2. Tel: 01-930 1552

Poets and politicians, actors and painters, and many, many kings and queens stare timelessly from gilded frames. But these heavy, traditional works are cleverly off-set by excellent quick sketches capturing the mood of a moment. Many of the portraits have helpful explanatory captions, and the attendants are always willing to fill in the gaps!

Tube: Charing Cross, Leicester Square
Open: Monday–Friday, 1000–1700, Saturday,
1000–1800, Sunday, 1400–1800

EXTRA . . . EXTRA . . . Often there is a chance to watch portraits being sketched by artists who set up their drawing boards just outside the Portrait Gallery. On a fine day look out for a different sort of artist drawing on the pavement with coloured chalks.

NATIONAL POSTAL MUSEUM, King Edward Building, King Edward Street, EC1. Tel: 01-432 3851

This is far more than simply a museum of stamps – it's one of the most comfortable, peaceful retreats in London. As well as seeing the 250,000 stamps covering all British issues from 1840 to the present day, you can read the original letter from Sir Rowland Hill (dated 1839) which outlines the Uniform Penny Postage scheme.There are also unique proofs of the Penny Black stamp and the Edward VIII Coronation set which was never issued. The staff are extremely helpful, and whether you're a stamp enthusiast or not they'll go out of their way to make your visit enjoyable.

Tube: St Paul's, Moorgate
Open: Monday–Friday, 0930–1630 (Friday, 1600)

EXTRA . . . EXTRA . . . Number 1, London. That was the postal address of Apsley House, now at 149 Piccadilly, W1, when the Duke of Wellington lived here in 1817–52.

NATURAL HISTORY MUSEUM, Cromwell
Road, SW7. Tel: 01-589 6323

Before you go into the Natural History Museum, take a
good look at the magnificent polychromatic stonework of
this impressive Victorian building, designed by Alfred
Waterhouse RA and built in 1873–80. Entering the
central hall through an ornate Romanesque doorway you
enter a different world, and it's one which seems almost
totally taken over by children! Huge reconstructions of
Triceratops and Diplodocus attract large numbers of
excited school-children happy to escape their teachers.
However, there are some corners of the museum where
adults can get some peace – and it really is a fascinating
place, with wonderful collections of birds and spiders!

Tube: South Kensington
Open: Free only Monday–Friday, 1630–1800, Saturday
and Sunday, 1700–1800

EXTRA . . . EXTRA . . . If you enjoy the architecture of
the Natural History Museum, take a look at two other
examples of Waterhouse's work: the headquarters of the
Prudential Assurance Company (1876) in Holborn, and
the City and Guilds Institute (1881) in Kensington.

OLD SPEECH ROOM GALLERY, Harrow
School, London Road, Harrow-on-the-Hill, Middlesex.
Tel: 01-422 2303

It is a well-known fact that this historic school boasts a list
of old boys that reads like a *Who's Who*, but did you

know it also has one of the best collections of butterflies in the world? The Old Speech Room Gallery is open to the public during term-time and as well as the butterflies, there are many other items of interest including paintings of former pupils including Lord Byron and Peel the Younger and an exhibition on perhaps the most famous of all, Winston Churchill. The rest of the school is only open to the public by guided tour (fee). (*See also Harrow Museum and Heritage Centre, page 110.*)

British Rail/Tube: Harrow-on-the-Hill
Open: Normally Monday and Friday–Sunday, 1430–1600, Tuesday and Thursday 1630–1800, but do phone in advance to check

---

EXTRA . . . EXTRA . . . It was at Harrow School that the modern game of squash rackets is said to have originated – played in the yard of the Head Master's House.

ORLEANS HOUSE GALLERY, Riverside, Twickenham, Middlesex. Tel: 01-892 0221

This villa was built in 1710 and named after Louis Philippe, Duc d'Orléans, who stayed here from 1815–17. The Octagon Room, a richly decorated baroque room designed by James Gibbs around 1720, and the carriage store, now converted into an art gallery, are all that remain of the original building. They hold exhibitions throughout the year. The house is set in a beautiful woodland garden overlooking the river.

British Rail: Twickenham
Tube: Richmond, then bus 270, 290 or 90B

Open: **House:** April–September, Tuesday–Saturday,
1300–1730, Sunday, 1400–1730, October–March,
Tuesday–Saturday, 1300–1630, Sunday,
1400–1630
Gardens: 0900–sunset

EXTRA . . . EXTRA . . . All the major Rugby Football
Union matches are played at Twickenham, so during the
season the town echoes with cheers from the stadium in
the appropriately named Rugby Road.

PERCIVAL DAVID FOUNDATION OF CHINESE ART, 53 Gordon Square, WC1.
Tel: 01-387 3909

In this excellent collection there are literally hundreds of
exquisite examples of Chinese ceramics – Yuan, Ming and
Ching dynasties – some of which once belonged to
Emperors.

Tube: Euston, Euston Square, Russell Square, Goodge
Street
Open: Monday, 1400–1700, Tuesday–Friday, 1030–1700,
Saturday, 1030–1300

EXTRA . . . EXTRA . . . In nearby Gower Street, WC1,
Charles Darwin lived in a house on the site of what is
now, aptly, the Biological Science Building of University
College.

THE PHOTOGRAPHER'S GALLERY, Halina House, 5 and 8 Great Newport Street, WC2. Tel: 01-831 1772

If you're interested in photography, don't miss this excellent gallery. It's in two sections; one part has a good small bookshop alongside a display area and the other uses the walls of a cafeteria for hanging space. In both exhibition areas you can, however, be sure to see fascinating and often stimulating photographs. There's also a library (for serious research by appointment) and a print room which houses a wide selection of images by new photographers as well as established professionals and recognized masters. All in all this gallery is a 'must' for photographers and would-be photographers of all kinds – even if you're only snap-happy!

Tube: Leicester Square
Open: Tuesday–Saturday, 1100–1900

EXTRA . . . EXTRA . . . If you're serious about taking photographs, you might consider presenting your work at an open submission – ask at the gallery for full details.

ROYAL AIR FORCE MUSEUM, Grahame Park Way, Hendon, NW9. Tel: 01-205 2266

Appropriately housed in two huge Belfast-truss hangars dating back to 1915, this magnificent collection of 40 aircraft and 12 galleries of related exhibits traces the history of the Royal Air Force from 1870 to the present day. It's set out in chronological order so you can work your way around from the Blériot Monoplane of 1909 to the supersonic Panavia Tornado and marvel at how technology has changed the face of flying machines. There's also an art gallery with paintings, including 'Hawker Harrier' by David Shepherd and 'Sunderland on Patrol' by Norman Hoad and, for anyone considering a career with the RAF, special audio-visual displays in Gallery 11.

Tube: Colindale
Open: Monday–Saturday, 1000–1800, Sunday,
     1400–1800

EXTRA . . . EXTRA . . . Ballooning used to be a popular pastime around the Welsh Harp in West Hendon. Indeed, back in 1862, Henry Coxwell and James Glaisher made a historic balloon flight from nearby Mill Hill to Biggleswade. The flight took six and a half hours and the two men took some 20 scientific instruments up with them.

ROYAL HOSPITAL CHELSEA MUSEUM,
Royal Hospital Chelsea, Royal Hospital Road, SW3.
Tel: 01-730 0161 ext. 203

This is only a small museum, housed in the Royal Hospital, but it's well worth a visit. It contains pictures, plans, medals and uniforms connected with the Royal Hospital. Don't miss the portrait of William Hiseland, who served 80 years in the army and died at the ripe old age of 112! The Royal Hospital, designed by Wren and built in the 1680s to look after old and disabled soldiers, is the home of the famous 'Chelsea Pensioners' with their distinguished scarlet coats and tricorn hats. The Chapel is open to the public and everyone is welcome to attend the Sunday service at 1100.

Tube: Sloane Square
Open: Monday–Saturday, 1000–1200, 1400–1600,
　　　　Sunday (April–September), 1400–1600

EXTRA . . . EXTRA . . . The Royal Hospital grounds are a delight to walk through. But as you do so, imagine how their peace is shattered by crowds of green-fingered gardeners when they become the venue for the colourful Chelsea Flower Show every May.

SCIENCE MUSEUM, Exhibition Road, South Kensington, SW7. Tel: 01-589 3456

There's so much to see and do in this enormous and exciting museum, which covers a whole seven acres and is dedicated to science and technology, that it's easy to come away feeling exhausted and completely frustrated. The best way to tackle it is by taking it slowly, enjoying each of the varied exhibits separately. Even if you only get to see *Puffing Billy*, the oldest locomotive in existence (dated 1813), or Stephenson's *Rocket* of 1829, you'll have enjoyed your visit. Right at the top is the Wellcome Museum of the History of Medicine, and downstairs there's a Children's Gallery with a galaxy of working models and push-button exhibits to make learning a positive pleasure. The museum also organizes free lectures and films (*see pages 22–23*).

Tube: South Kensington
Open: Monday–Saturday, 1000–1800
Sunday, 1430–1800

EXTRA . . . EXTRA . . . While you're in the area walk to Queen's Gate, SW7, and stop at Baden-Powell House, which is full of mementoes of Lord Baden-Powell, the founder of the Scout Movement who died in 1941 (open: daily, 0800–2230, tel: 01-584 7030).

SERPENTINE GALLERY, Kensington Gardens, W2. Tel: 01-402 6075

This small gallery must have the most perfect setting, situated close to the Albert Memorial in Kensington Gardens (*see page 160*). Once an old teahouse, it today specializes in contemporary works of art which are always well exhibited, often with helpful notes. As the gallery closes between exhibitions do telephone to see what's on.

Tube: Knightsbridge, South Kensington
Open: Monday–Sunday; roughly 1000–1800, but do telephone for times – they change according to the hours of daylight!

EXTRA . . . EXTRA . . . Look out for the boundary stone of the old Metropolitan Borough of Paddington (MBP) in the northern part of Kensington Gardens.

SIR JOHN SOANE'S MUSEUM, 13 Lincoln's Inn Fields, WC2. Tel: 01-405 2107 (*see also walk 1, page 241*)

Eccentric is the best word to describe this amazing collection of antiquities and works of art put together by Sir John Soane, the architect. Soane, the son of a country builder, was very keen on playing architectural games, as you'll soon discover. He built the house as a museum for his vases, urns, busts, paintings, and other collectors' items. When he died in 1837 he bequeathed it to the nation on condition that nothing in it was removed or changed. Well, here it is! In the Picture Room the walls are layered with folding planes which when opened reveal paintings and drawings. In the Library, clever placing of mirrors makes it look as though there are extra rooms. One good way to see the museum is by the public lecture tour on Saturdays at 1430, but it's worth a visit any time. (*See also Dulwich Park Extra, page 153.*)

Tube: Holborn
Open: Tuesday–Saturday, 1000–1700

EXTRA . . . EXTRA . . . Sir John Soane is best remembered for his work on The Bank of England, Threadneedle Street, EC2. However, it was redesigned in 1925–39 by Sir Herbert Baker and only the outer walls of Soane's original building remain. Stand outside the Bank of England, the 'Old Lady of Threadneedle Street', and you're right in the heart of financial London with the International Futures Exchange, the Stock Exchange and the headquarters of all the major national and international banks around.

TATE GALLERY, Millbank, SW1. Tel: 01-821 1313

The Tate Gallery houses major collections of British paintings of all periods. There is a large collection of Constable's work, as well as many excellent paintings by Blake and Sargent. Fascinating too are the galleries of 16th- and 17th-century paintings which include John Bettes' *Man in a Black Cap*, 1545. The Tate also has an important collection of modern foreign sculptures, prints and paintings, including the work of Georges Braque, Marc Chagall, Oskar Kokoschka and Matisse. In 1987, the Queen opened a new extension to the Tate, the Clore Gallery. This two-storey L-shaped building, designed by architect James Stirling, houses the National Turner Collection.

Tube: Pimlico
Open: Monday–Saturday, 1000–1750
Sunday, 1400–1750

EXTRA . . . EXTRA . . . A Henry Moore sculpture, *Interlocking Piece*, can be seen beside the busy main road just outside the Tate.

VICTORIA AND ALBERT MUSEUM, Cromwell Road, SW7. Tel: 01-589 6371

This exciting museum of fine and applied arts is packed with so much to see from all countries and periods that it almost has to be approached in sections, each section demanding a separate visit – European and Oriental, armour, glass, pottery, furniture. There are collections of sculpture, water colours, miniatures and lots more – a veritable treasure-trove. Right in the heart of the museum is an outdoor quadrangle which provides a comfortable place during the summer to eat a packed lunch. For a special treat, make for the sixth floor of the Henry Cole wing – the view over the rooftops of Knightsbridge is simply fantastic.

Tube: South Kensington
Open: Monday–Thursday and Saturday, 1000–1730,
Sunday, 1430–1730
Note: The Victoria and Albert Museum asks rather
forcefully for 'voluntary contributions', but you
are able to enter for free if you wish.

EXTRA . . . EXTRA . . . The Victoria and Albert Museum, colloquially known as the 'V and A', is in the area of London known as Knightsbridge. The name Knightsbridge originates from the days of the crusaders, when the local West Bourn river was spanned by a stone bridge built by Edward the Confessor. Two Knights were said to have fought on the bridge, and to have fallen into the river and drowned.

WALLACE COLLECTION, Hertford House, Manchester Square, W1. Tel: 01-935 0687

The Wallace family collection of armour, French furniture and fine paintings, including *The Laughing Cavalier* by Frans Hals, was brought over to England from Paris by Richard Wallace, 4th Marquess of Hertford, and bequeathed to the nation by his wife, Lady Wallace, in

1897. Unfortunately, there's no printed guide to the collection, but uniformed staff, who seem to be present at every corner, are very willing to pass on their expert knowledge.

Tube: Baker Street, Bond Street, Marble Arch
Open: Monday–Friday, 1000–1700, Sunday, 1400–1700

EXTRA . . . EXTRA . . . Michael Faraday (1791–1867), a remarkable scientific genius, worked as a bookseller's apprentice at 48 Blandford Street, W1.

WHITECHAPEL ART GALLERY,
80 Whitechapel High Street, E1. Tel: 01-377 0107

You can never be quite sure what you'll find in this art gallery with its frequently changing exhibitions, but you can always be sure it'll be of a high standard. The gallery specializes in modern art and, in the past, exhibitions have included the works of Hepworth, Moore and Hockney. Most exhibitions are free but occasionally there's a charge. The gallery also has talks and presentations and there's an excellent café serving light refreshments.

Tube: Aldgate East
Open: Tuesday–Sunday, 1100–1700, Wednesday open
             until 2000

EXTRA . . . EXTRA . . . Virtually next door is Bloom's Kosher Restaurant, famous world-wide for its delicious salt beef.

WILLIAM MORRIS GALLERY, Water House, Lloyd Park, Forest Road, Walthamstow, E17. Tel: 01-527 5544 ext. 4390

Fittingly, Water House (built *c*. 1750) was for a time the home of William Morris (1834–96) – designer, publisher and socialist – to whom it is now devoted. In it you can see a fascinating collection illustrating the life, work and beliefs of this important and influential Victorian. His passion was a 'hatred of modern civilization', while his ambition was to re-establish the ideals of what he viewed as the idyllic pre-industrial age. Influenced by art critic John Ruskin, a champion of the Gothic revival, Morris founded workshops which celebrated craftsmanship. In the gallery you can see examples of both his own work and products from his workshops. Look out for a set of wood blocks used for printing 'Wandle Chintz' and an elegant 'Sussex' rush-seated chair made *c*. 1868.

Tube: Walthamstow Central
Open: Tuesday–Saturday, 1000–1300 and 1400–1700.
        Also on the first Sunday of each month.
        Note: at the time of going to press the future of
        this gallery is uncertain, do telephone before you
        visit.

EXTRA . . . EXTRA . . . Water House is situated in a small park which has a pretty duck-filled stretch of water. But you'd have to have a vivid imagination to get any idea how Walthamstow looked when Morris lived here – it was then just a pleasant village in the Lea Valley countryside!

CHAPTER FIVE

Parks and Open Spaces

ALEXANDRA PARK, Wood Green, N22.
Tel: 01-883 0809

This park was once the site of Tottenham Wood Farm, and as you wander through the 480 acres of green and undulating parkland it's easy to think back to those days. Although there are no farm animals now, you can still soak up all that fresh country air. Walk up the hill to Alexandra Palace, an international exhibition hall, and enjoy the far-reaching views over London. You can usually catch a sporting event in the park at weekends – although the standard varies!

Tube: Finsbury Park, then bus W3
Open: all the time

EXTRA . . . EXTRA . . . The world's first regular television broadcasts were made by the BBC from Alexandra Palace from 2 November 1936.

BARNES BRIDGE TO HAMMERSMITH BRIDGE (north bank)

The elegant houses on the waterfront near Barnes Bridge railway station are worth taking a look at (one once belonged to Gustav Holst, composer of *The Planets Suite*) before you take the footbridge across the Thames. The pathway east along the north bank will take you through an area of lawned terraces, created to provide a good view of the annual Boat Race (*page 205*). For a short distance the route leaves the waterfront and cuts through a small housing estate into Edensor Gardens, then on into Pumping Station Road. The warehouses here are a very real contrast to the beautiful houses and popular pubs just five minutes' walk away – so keep going!

British Rail: Barnes Bridge
Tube: Hammersmith
Open: all the time

EXTRA . . . EXTRA . . . On your way to Hammersmith tube look out for a pub called The Dove. Here, in a small room upstairs, James Thompson composed 'Rule Britannia'.

BATTERSEA PARK, Battersea, SW11. Tel: 01-228 2798

An extremely varied park on the south bank of the Thames, just next to Battersea Power Station (but don't let that put you off – it has its own beauty!). Attractive areas such as lakes with bankside sculptures by Henry Moore and Barbara Hepworth, and recreation facilities have been skilfully combined to provide something for everyone. There's a small enclosure with deer and pea-cocks, which delight young children, as do the many geese and ducks which flock in to gobble up crumbs of bread.

Look out for the Peace Pagoda and the herb garden. The more active will appreciate the tennis courts, boating, bowling and running track (though a fee is payable for these), while those who prefer a gentle stroll should make for the river bank and enjoy the view across the water to Chelsea. Battersea Park is also the site of many south bank open-air activities, the best known of which is the Easter Parade (*see page 207*), although others take place throughout the year; keep an eye on the local press.

British Rail: Battersea Park
Bus: 137
Open: daily until dusk

EXTRA ... EXTRA ... Asparagus was cultivated on this riverside site before it became a park in the mid-19th century.

BLACKFRIARS BRIDGE TO WESTMINSTER BRIDGE (north bank)

The north bank of the River Thames, so steeped in historic interest, is a fascinating place to explore. A particularly enjoyable walk is alongside Victoria Embankment which runs between Westminster and Blackfriars, a riverside route offering some splendid views. The road was first proposed by Christopher Wren after the Great Fire but wasn't built until 1864–70 with land reclaimed from the river. Obviously you can approach the walk from either direction but save the best bit until last and start at Blackfriars Bridge. Steps lead down from the bridge, originally a toll bridge completed in 1790, to Victoria Embankment. The walk takes you past three ships moored on the river: HMS *President* and HMS *Chrysanthemum*, two sloops from the First World War, and HMS *Wellington*, the floating livery hall of the Honourable Company of Master Mariners. Across the road to your right is The Temple (*see page 67*), London's legal quarter. As you continue beneath Waterloo Bridge, the huge Cleopatra's Needle seems to leap out to greet you. Standing 68½ feet high, this granite obelisk dates back to 1500 B.C. and is the oldest monument in London. A plaque describes its history and eventful journey from Egypt to England. Opposite are Victoria Embankment Gardens (*see page 170*), host to summer-time band concerts and art exhibitions. The walkway takes you beneath Hungerford footbridge and now Big Ben (*see page 34*) and the Houses of Parliament (*see page 184*) are clearly in view. The river is buzzing with activity for this last stretch of the walk – Westminster Pier is the major launching point for riverboat cruises upriver to Kew, Putney, Richmond and Hampton Court and downriver to the Tower and Greenwich. The riverside walk ends at the Houses of Parliament, but you can always cross Westminster Bridge and continue along the south bank (*see Lambeth Bridge to Tower Bridge, page 161*).

Tube: Blackfriars, Embankment, Westminster
Open: all the time

EXTRA . . . EXTRA . . . Thames is the second-oldest place name in England, the oldest is Kent. Although it's not know quite how it got the name, records show that Caesar called the river Tamesis.

BLACKHEATH, SE3. Tel: 01-858 1692

This common covers 167 acres and links with Greenwich Park (*page 152*) on its northern edge. Every acre is rich in historical connections – this is where the Danes camped in 1011, as did highwaymen and rebels in later years. It is also where James I first introduced golf to England and where Charles II was welcomed by the citizens of London after his restoration to the throne. But it's still very much alive today with people walking, flying kites, picnicking and playing sport. You can combine the visit with Greenwich and Ranger's House (*see page 53*).

British Rail: Blackheath, Maze Hill
Tube: New Cross, New Cross Gate, then bus 53
Open: all the time

EXTRA . . . EXTRA . . . In the 18th century there were only two cottages in Blackheath but in 1849 the railway was opened. The heath suddenly came within very easy reach of central London for well-to-do Victorians and a thriving village quickly grew.

BROCKWELL PARK, Dulwich Road, SE24

A visit to Brockwell Park, situated between Brixton and Dulwich, can be combined well with a trip to Electric Avenue market (*page 82*) or Dulwich Park (*page 152*). In the midst of its large open green area, which is popular with local people, there's a secret walled garden. Immaculate old yew hedges and hundreds of colourful herbaceous plants make it both an interesting and tranquil spot to seek out. Originally the kitchen garden of a private manor house built in 1810, the walled garden has a sense of privacy which contrasts well with the expansive and very public quality of its parkland setting.

British Rail: Herne Hill
Open: daily, 0700–dusk

EXTRA . . . EXTRA . . . Brockwell Hall now does service as the park restaurant!

BUSHY PARK, Middlesex

Lying on either side of Hampton Court Palace, Bushy Park and Hampton Court Gardens (*page 157*) cover around 1,099 acres. Bushy Park is the less formal of the two, with all sorts of visitors from dog-walkers to sunbathers and cricket players. You'll find a lot of picnickers here in the summer too. Look out for the impressive avenue of horse chestnut trees with the fountain and bronze statue of Diana the huntress standing at the southern end, and Bushy Park House, once lived in by William IV when he was Duke of Clarence. And of course, not to be missed are the deer and sheep which roam around freely and are really quite tame.

British Rail: Teddington
Tube: Richmond, then bus 33
Open: daily 0630–2400

EXTRA . . . EXTRA . . . The Chestnut Avenue used to be a popular place for Londoners celebrating Chestnut

Sunday (Sunday nearest 11 May). They came to picnic and admire the beautiful blossom. Why not follow the old tradition yourself?

CANAL WALK, Uxbridge to Mile End

Stretching from Uxbridge to Mile End and mostly hidden from view, Regent's Canal is an excellent, often forgotten, place to take a walk. It passes through basins and parks; past restaurants and museums; through the zoo and a market; under bridges and beside docks. A stroll along its banks is like walking through a kaleidoscope, so many images briefly present themselves then disappear. The canal goes through some of the poorest parts of London as well as through its more expensive areas. Sometimes it's flanked by modern architecture, and sometimes by buildings from its industrial past – but always it's fascinating. There are entrances and exits all along the route, so you can walk as much or as little as you want.

Tube: Uxbridge, Northolt, Greenford, Warwick Avenue, Camden Town, King's Cross, Angel, Mile End

Open: Times vary. West from Kensal Green there is free access but on other sections the towpaths are, in general, open from 0900–dusk.

EXTRA . . . EXTRA . . . Canals were built and owned by independent companies. But in 1929, London's canal companies joined together to form the Grand Union

Canal Company. Later, in 1947, the waterways of Britain were nationalized under the Transport Act, and since 1962 they've been under the control of the British Waterways Board (telephone 01-262 6711).

CHISWICK HOUSE GARDENS, Burlington
Lane, W4. Tel: 01-995 0508

Chiswick House Gardens are a perfect place to take a quiet stroll. Designed by William Kent for Lord Burlington, the gardens are a romantic green haven. Lawns are dotted with statues and pathways, flanked by high hedges, and unexpectedly with a temple or obelisk. A classical bridge spans the picturesque stretch of river which passes through the gardens and which is home for a variety of water fowl. To the east you'll find the Royal and Italian gardens, the orangery, Inigo Jones Gateway and the Conservatory, while in the south there's a cricket ground. All in all, there's plenty to enjoy here for all the family. Nearby is Hogarth's House (*see page 111*).

Tube: Hammersmith then bus 290
British Rail: Chiswick
Open: daily. Times vary slightly, but are roughly
          daylight hours

EXTRA . . . EXTRA . . . Chiswick House Gardens form a beautiful setting for Chiswick House itself (fee to enter), built in 1725–9 as a showcase for Lord Burlington's private art collection. From the Gardens you can see many of its main design features, including the octagonal central dome which is flanked by four obelisk-shaped chimney stacks.

CLAPHAM COMMON, Clapham, SW4

Bleak in winter when its flatness is exaggerated, Clapham Common becomes the centre of numerous activities during the summer months. In bygone days it was a patch of overgrown waste land, pasturage for sheep; today it's a popular venue for fairs, sports and even gymkhanas. If you are there on a Sunday look out for miniature power-boat enthusiasts racing their models on the pond. On the corner of the common stands the parish church of Holy Trinity – an impressive building in its cluster of trees, particularly during the summer. The nearby water fountain was originally erected at the City approach to London Bridge in 1884. However, its weight caused the arches of the bridge to crack, so in 1895 it was moved to its present site on Clapham Common.

Tube: Clapham Common, Clapham South
Open: all the time

EXTRA ... EXTRA ... In The Chase, a street off Clapham Common Northside, may be seen one of the earliest type of Victorian letter-boxes.

CRYSTAL PALACE PARK, Norwood, SE19.
Tel: 01-778 7148

If you've ever fancied hunting for dinosaurs this is the place to do it! There are no less than 20 lurking in the undergrowth or emerging from the depths of murky pools. Made for the Great Exhibition of 1851, these plaster prehistoric monsters are extremely popular with small children. However, if dinosaur hunting isn't your particular hobby there are plenty of other things to do in Crystal Palace park. How about a go on the boating lake, a visit to the small zoo, or a run across its acres of open space?

British Rail: Crystal Palace
Tube: Brixton, then bus 137
Open: daily

EXTRA . . . EXTRA . . . From the park you can get a view of the athletics stadium. You might even spot a famous sports personality.

DULWICH PARK, Dulwich Village, SE21. Tel: 01-693 5737

Wonderful displays of rhododendrons and azaleas make Dulwich Park, a favourite garden of King George V's wife Queen Mary, a colourful place to visit. There's also a well-stocked aviary and a pretty lake with a sculpture by Barbara Hepworth. When you visit the park, make sure you've time to browse round the village – it's very picturesque and expensive!

British Rail: North Dulwich, West Dulwich
Open: 0730–dusk

EXTRA . . . EXTRA . . . On the village side of the park, in College Road, is the Dulwich Picture Gallery (fee to enter), which is an important and interesting piece of architecture designed in 1811–14 by Sir John Soane (*see also Sir John Soane's Museum, page 135*). Look out for the mausoleum which forms the central axis for two wings of almshouses on the west side of the building.

EPPING FOREST, Essex

Once a royal hunting forest (look out for Elizabeth I's hunting lodge) these beautiful woods make an excellent day-trip. Baldwin's Hill Pond and The Lost Pond are picturesque picnic spots, but if you want to leave the main tracks do take a map and compass there are some 6,000 acres to explore and although the forest is never at any time more than a mile from a road it's still very easy to get lost. If you're good at map-reading you may be able to find two ancient sites, Loughton Camp and Ambersbury Banks, each around 2,000 years old. A variety of wildlife can be spotted, but the deer have been driven into reserves near Theydon Bois.

Tube: Snaresbrook
Open: all the time

EXTRA . . . EXTRA . . . If you visit the forest in autumn – a particularly spectacular season, when the trees posi-

tively glow orange – be brave and go edible-fungi-hunting!
. . . but do take a good guide book.

GREEN PARK, SW1

Green Park is exactly that – green! There are no colourful
flowerbeds here, just grassland and trees. The 53-acre
park has played host to many spectacular events since it
was enclosed by Henry VIII as a deer park; desperate
duels have been fought and passers-by, including Horace
Walpole, held up here by highwaymen. There have also
been fantastic firework displays in the past, but today it is
simply a pleasant green place to sit and a very enjoyable
short-cut from Piccadilly on one side to Buckingham
Palace (*see page 36*) on the other. A feature of note is the
Broad Walk which leads to the Victoria Memorial.

Tube: Green Park
Open: daily 0500–2400

EXTRA . . . EXTRA . . . It's thought that the park was
once a burial ground for leper women from the hospital
of St James's.

GREENWICH PARK, Greenwich, SE10

Greenwich Park was enclosed in 1433 by order of Henry
VI and is the oldest of the Royal Parks. In 1515 a special
order was passed that the park should be stocked with
deer, and you can still see a herd of fallow deer roaming

around. There's also a pond with wildfowl and a bird sanctuary. As you wander through the park and flower gardens take time to admire the views. The park rises to a hill some 155 feet above the river where you'll find the Old Royal Observatory and General Wolfe monument. (*See also London Marathon, page 210.*)

British Rail: Maze Hill
Tube: New Cross, New Cross Gate, then bus 177
Open: all the time

EXTRA . . . EXTRA . . . General James Wolfe, who was killed in action, aged only 32, after leading the successful attack on Quebec in 1759, lived with his parents in Macartney House, facing Greenwich Park.

HAMMERSMITH BRIDGE TO BARNES BRIDGE FOOTPATH (south bank)

This delightful riverside footpath, along the Thames' south bank, can be combined with the north bank walk from Barnes Bridge to Hammersmith (*page 143*) to make a circular route. Starting at Hammersmith Bridge, the little-known leafy public right of way closely hugs the river bank. The view across the Thames to warehouses, boathouses, pubs and private homes is fascinating and there's plenty to see on the river itself – enthusiastic oarsmen seem to be on the water from dawn till dusk, every day of the year!

British Rail: Barnes Bridge
Tube: Hammersmith
Open: all the time

EXTRA . . . EXTRA . . . The village of Barnes is well worth a short detour (about five minutes' walk from Barnes Bridge). Look out for the picturesque village green and duck pond.

HAMPSTEAD HEATH, Hampstead, NW3

This stretch of unspoilt heathland is the ideal place to get away from it all. It covers about 790 acres, so it's easy to get lost. You'll find some lovely walks over sandy hills, through woodland and across lush grass. Areas of the Heath to look for are Whitestone Pond, popular for sailing boats, and nearby The Vale of Health, so called because all the inhabitants of this hamlet survived the Great Plague of 1665. Parliament Hill to the east of the Heath is a favourite place for flying kites and children's parties in the summer. There's plenty of space for all sorts of sporting activities, from cricket to horseriding. Look out for wildlife too. It's well worth spending a whole day here and bringing a picnic for lunch. (*See also Open Air Art Exhibitions, page 23.*)

British Rail: Hampstead Heath
Tube: Hampstead (then walk up Heath Street)
Open: all the time

EXTRA . . . EXTRA . . . In the 18th century Hampstead was a fashionable spa resort. The healing mineral water was taken from a local well and sold in flasks to visitors. Hence two of the street names – Flask Walk and Well Walk.

HAMPTON COURT GARDENS, Hampton Court Road, East Molesey, Middlesex.

There is a charge to go into the palace, built during Henry VIII's reign for Cardinal Wolsey, but the extensive gardens and deer park are absolutely free – they make an excellent summer afternoon trip. The palace was restyled by Christopher Wren and the grounds were planned as part of the whole design. There are many old yew trees, a number of beautiful walled gardens, and a very impressive ancient vine whose roots, tradition has it, reach down to the Thames. Look out for the Tudor tennis courts built by Henry VIII and still used today. The maze must be mentioned; although there is a small charge, it's a good place to lose children! (*See also Bushy Park, page 148.*)

British Rail: Hampton Court
Tube: Hammersmith, then bus 267
Open: daily, 0700–an hour before dusk

EXTRA . . . EXTRA . . . When workmen were repairing rafters in Westminster Hall, New Palace Yard, SW1, they discovered tennis balls which had been lost in Henry VIII's day!

HOLLAND PARK, W8

This extremely pretty park, once the private park of Holland House, a Jacobean mansion largely destroyed in 1941 by bombing, is very well worth going out of your way to visit. Semi-tame rabbits, which delight young visitors, are everywhere, and in the woodland area squirrels abound. Look out for the peacocks, which never fail to give a spectacular display and, as in most parks, there are lots of ducks. Holland Park can also boast owls and green woodpeckers and there are said to be 3,000 species of trees and plants. The old Orangery, surrounded by beautiful rose gardens, and the Ice House now house changing exhibitions which are free.

Tube: High Street Kensington, Holland Park
Open: daily, until dusk

EXTRA ... EXTRA ... When Holland House was owned by the 3rd Lord Holland (1773–1840) it became very popular with well-known people of the day. Macaulay described it as the 'favourite resort of wits and beauties, of painters and poets, of scholars, philosophers and statesmen'.

HYDE PARK, W1, W2, SW7

Hyde Park is a huge expanse of greenery right in the heart of the capital. For the shopper it offers an alternative way of getting from Oxford Street's shops to Knightsbridge's boutiques. This scenic route passes via the Serpentine (spot the swimmers in winter!), Speakers' Corner (*see page 29*), Ranger's Lodge and Rotten Row (*see Riding Horse Parade, page 219*). It's fair to say that it's best to concentrate while you walk as danger does lurk in the park in the form of galloping horses, bicycles and even cars. Londoners use Hyde Park as a lunch-time picnic place in the summer. Particularly favoured are the benches alongside the Serpentine, where pigeons and ducks vie with each other for dropped crumbs. (*See also London to Brighton Bike Race, page 212, and the Veteran Car Run, page 231.*)

Tube: Marble Arch, Lancaster Gate, Knightsbridge, Hyde Park Corner
Open: all the time

EXTRA . . . EXTRA . . . On a fine day look out for pavement artists near Marble Arch. With a few pieces of coloured chalk and a lot of expertise they produce amazing portraits and landscapes – only to see them washed away with the first shower.

JUBILEE GARDENS, South Bank, SE1 (*see also Walk 3, page 247*)

Opened to celebrate the Queen's Silver Jubilee year in 1977, these gardens on the bank of the Thames offer a perfect picnic spot. Children love the brightly coloured and imaginatively laid-out play area, and the adults can sit on the many benches. The only thing to watch out for is the pigeons, ever eager for a tasty morsel! There's music here at lunchtimes in the summer.

Tube: Waterloo
Open: all the time

EXTRA . . . EXTRA . . . If you notice people stopping and looking at the paving stones along The Queen's Walk by the gardens, there's a very good reason for it. Carved in the stone are words of poems, songs and ditties all relating to London. Authors range from Wordsworth to Spike Milligan.

KENSINGTON GARDENS, W2, W8

Kensington Gardens cover about 275 acres of what was once (along with Hyde Park (*see page 158*)) part of Henry VIII's hunting grounds. Its beautiful flower beds (particularly colourful is the Sunken Garden attached to Kensington Palace), large open spaces and boating facilities make it very popular with Londoners who flock here at the weekend. It contains many statues and sculptures including a pretty figure of Peter Pan and a magnificent lakeside work by Barbara Hepworth. But most famous of all the park's sculptures is undoubtedly the Albert Memorial (Kensington Gore, SW7). Designed by Sir George Gilbert Scott, the Albert Memorial is an extraordinarily elaborate piece of Victoriana. The intricate detail is piled high in true Gothic tradition. At the angles of the pedestal are groups representing Agriculture, Manufacture, Commerce, and Engineering; while at the bottom four groups of carvings represent Africa (a camel), Asia (an elephant), Europe (a bull), and America (a bison). Clustered above are hundreds of figures representing just about everything! Built between 1863 and 1872 it is, as its name suggests, a memorial to Prince Albert, Queen Victoria's consort who died of typhoid in 1861. (*See also Serpentine Gallery, page 134.*)

Tube: High Street Kensington, Lancaster Gate
Open: all the time

EXTRA . . . EXTRA . . . In Charles II's time the gardens were very popular with the fashionable set who would parade in the hope of being noticed by the King.

LAMBETH BRIDGE TO TOWER BRIDGE
(south bank)

London's River Thames is slowly becoming recognized as an important amenity for residents and visitors alike. Its south bank has, over the last few years, been gradually developed and opened up to the public; it's now possible to walk, with only a couple of short detours away from the water, all the way from Lambeth Bridge to Tower Bridge. A distinctive landmark beside Lambeth Bridge is Lambeth Palace (not open to the public), the London home of the Archbishop of Canterbury. It has a less well known neighbour, the Museum of Garden History (*see page 120*). The Thames-side walk continues past St Thomas's Hospital with its pretty garden (note the moving fountain by sculptor Naum Gabo) just beside Westminster Bridge. From here can be gained perhaps the finest view of the Houses of Parliament (*see page 184*) and Big Ben (*see page 34*). Next, the walk passes beside County Hall and the Shell Building and on under Hungerford footbridge (popular with buskers) to the Royal Festival Hall (*see page 28*) and the Hayward Gallery (fee); across the water can be seen London's famous Savoy Hotel. Walk under Waterloo Bridge and pass on your right the National Theatre (*see page 23*) and London Weekend Television's tower; and on towards another distinctive tower, known, for reasons which will become immediately obvious, as the 'Oxo Tower' (built in 1928, it was an early advertising gimmick). Walking beside decaying buildings and modern office blocks and with spectacular views across the Thames to St Paul's Cathedral (*see page 64*) you'll soon reach Blackfriars Bridge. Cross the road here and take the steps which lead down to the water front. The views across the Thames along this next stretch are fascinating; they include the spires of St Andrew-by-the-Wardrobe, St Bernet, St Nicholas and St Mary Somerset. The walk itself passes beside a pub and then continues on past the monolithic hulk of Bankside Power Station. Another small detour takes you away from the river and through the gloomy warehouses around Clink Street (site of one of London's infamous prisons) and the site of Shakespeare's Globe Theatre. It's an interesting area packed with history and atmosphere. Make your way to the haven of Southwark Cathedral (*see page 66*), and after wandering through its small garden you'll emerge onto London Bridge. Cross the road and descend a couple of steps which appear to lead into a glossy office block called No 1 London Bridge; in fact they lead to newly-developed St Martins Walk. this pleasant promenade, with its views across to the City including the Monument and the top of Lloyd's (*see page 185*), leads to Hays Galleria. Here a most unusual ship-cum-sea monster takes centre stage in a glazed vaulted shopping arcade. Continue walking beside the river and you'll quickly reach HMS *Belfast* (fee) – the last surviving cruiser from the Second World War. You must now once again leave the waterside and walk down Vine Lane to Tooley Street. Turn left and it is just a few minutes' stroll to Tower Bridge with its excellent panorama of the Tower of London.

Tube: south bank – Waterloo, London Bridge; north bank – Westminster, Embankment, Blackfriars, Tower Hill
Open: all the time

EXTRA ... EXTRA ... Tower Bridge (EC3) is a popular spot with tourists wanting a holiday snapshot. However, its attractive Victorian Gothic structure cleverly disguises a powerful hydraulically-operated drawbridge (designed by Jones and Wolfe Barry in 1894) which is lifted to allow large ships and high-masted sailing boats to pass.

LINCOLN'S INN FIELDS, WC2 (*see also Walk 2, page 243*)

This huge square is a wonderful haven from the busy traffic, office blocks and bustling crowds. There are lots of trees which look magnificent in the autumn and which serve to screen off areas. In the centre of the square, an octagonal covered area with seats provides a handy shelter for those watching netball matches on the two nearby courts. There are also band concerts, tennis courts and a small cafeteria – it all adds up to a popular lunchtime venue. (*See also Pancake Day, page 202 and Sir John Soane Museum, page 135.*)

Tube: Aldwych, Holborn, Chancery Lane (not Sundays)
Open: daily

EXTRA ... EXTRA ... Spencer Perceval lived at 59–60 Lincoln's Inn Fields. In 1807 he was Chancellor of the

Exchequer; two years later he was Prime Minister, but in May 1812 he was assassinated in the lobby of the House of Commons.

OSTERLEY PARK, Isleworth, Middlesex. Tel: 01-560 3918

The original manor house was built by Sir Thomas Gresham in the 16th century and was visited by Elizabeth I in 1576. During the mid-18th century Robert Adam was asked to redesign the building and the original structure was encased by the new walls seen today. There is a charge to go into the house, but the stables, which are the only unaltered architecture, can be seen for free. Set in extensive parkland, Osterley is worth a Sunday trip. The beautiful lake has many interesting species of geese and ducks, and scattered in the grounds are many unusual trees.

Tube: Osterley
Open: daily, 1000–dusk

EXTRA . . . EXTRA . . . Francis Child bought Osterley in 1711 but he never lived here. However, it stayed in the family until it was presented to the nation by the 9th Earl of Jersey in 1949. Francis Child was one of the City's first bankers and his original bank at 1 Fleet Street, EC4, is thought to be one of the oldest in the country. It stands opposite Temple Bar.

PRIMROSE HILL, NW8. Tel: 01-486 7905

Climb the grassy slope of Primrose Hill for a spectacular panorama across London. Many of the capital's most famous landmarks can be clearly seen: the Nat West Tower, the dome of St Paul's Cathedral (*see page 64*), St Pancras Station (*see page 63*), the high tower of Guy's Hospital, Bankside Power Station, Senate House (University of London), Centre Point, Telecom Tower, Victoria Tower, Houses of Parliament (*see page 184*), Crystal Palace (*see page 152*) TV mast, Westminster Cathedral (*see page 71*) and Battersea Power Station. But scan the middle distance and you have perhaps the best view of all – of London Zoo. From this excellent vantage point you can see the distinctive tensile structure of the aviary and the green copper roofs of the elephant house. Definitely a view not to be missed!

Tube: Camden Town
Open: daily

EXTRA . . . EXTRA . . . Primrose Hill has some of the best up-currents of any of London's open spaces. So take a kite and be prepared to chase it!

REGENT'S PARK, NW1

This is one of London's most pleasant parks, always full of flowers and plants. It's surrounded on three sides by Nash terraces and by the Regent's Canal (*see Canal Walk, page 149*) on the fourth. A favourite spot is the Queen Mary Gardens in the inner circle of the park. These

gardens are a delight in June when they overflow with
perfumed roses. There's also an open air theatre, a
bandstand and a mobile puppet theatre. No shortage of
things to do and see with football pitches, cricket nets,
rugby pitches and tennis courts. And don't miss the
boating lake with the friendly ducks. (*See also Harness
Horse Parade, page 208.*)

Tube: Regent's Park, Camden Town, Great Portland
Street
Open: daily until dusk

EXTRA . . . EXTRA . . . You can get a very good view
of the animals in London Zoo in the north-east corner of
the park. Walk up Broad Walk to see the deer and
wolves, then turn left into the Outer Circle and past the
main entrance spotting the giraffes and monkeys. Complete the triangle, catching good glimpses of all the other
animals.

RICHMOND PARK, Richmond, Surrey.
Tel: 01 940 0654

This is the largest of the Royal parks, covering 2500 acres.
It's the ideal place for a good, long walk in the countryside. The park was enclosed by Charles I in 1637 and is
famed for its red and fallow deer. You don't have to look
far for them either. There are also golf courses, lakes for
model boats, and plenty of space for sports of all kind.
The Isabella Plantation is a wooded, enclosed garden full
of azaleas and magnolias. Two buildings of note are White
Lodge, built in 1727 by George II and now the home of

the Royal Ballet Junior School, and Pembroke Lodge, which serves as the cafeteria.

Tube: Richmond, then bus 71
Open: daily, 0700–half an hour before dusk

EXTRA . . . EXTRA . . . This is the place to go for beautiful views. The view of the Thames Valley which you get from Terrace Gardens has been painted by artists including Turner and Reynolds. Richmond in Virginia, USA, was named after Richmond, Surrey, because of the similarity of the views. To get to Terrace Gardens leave Richmond Park by the Richmond Gate exit and walk up Richmond Hill. The gardens are on your left.

THE ROOKERY, Streatham Common North, SW16

Once part of a private estate, The Rookery is an unexpected and little-known gem in the heart of south London. This three-acre garden contains one of the oldest cedars in the country, a really delighful water garden, and many beautiful ornamental trees. During the summer it bursts into life with a riot of colourful flower-beds. Except, that is, the White Garden. Walled and refined, the White Garden, as its name suggests, is planted only with white plants. Flowering bulbs of every description, shrubs, roses and a wide variety of herbaceous plants are lovingly cared for – the result is simple and very elegant.

British Rail: Streatham
Open: daily, 0900–dusk

EXTRA . . . EXTRA . . . The Rookery is situated on the edge of Streatham Common (a good place for a windy walk) which includes a pleasant wooded area.

RUSSELL SQUARE, WC1 (*see also Walk 2, page 243*)

A well-known square conveniently close to the British Museum (*see page 99*), the University of London and Tottenham Court Road. Plenty of trees, rather unusual fountains and lots of grass make this a popular place for munching sandwiches with tourists, students and office workers.

Tube: Russell Square
Open: daily

EXTRA . . . EXTRA . . . Two law reformers lived in Russell Square. At 50–51 lived Lord Thomas Denman, who was in favour of the abolition of the death penalty for forgery, while at number 21 lived Sir Samuel Romilly, who wanted to reduce the number of crimes punishable by death.

ST JAMES'S PARK, The Mall, SW1 (*see also Walk 1, page 241*) Tel: 01-930 1793

A picturesque park spanning the area between Whitehall and Buckingham Palace (*see page 36*) with unusual and beautiful views of both. Dominated by a winding lake it is a popular place to feed ducks and pigeons. Along the water's edge thoughtfully provided plaques describe the variety of ducks which can be seen. More spectacular, however, are the pelicans, which glide majestically past the many tourists and office workers who, particularly in late spring and summer, flock to enjoy the colourful banks of flowers.

Tube: St James's Park
Open: daily, 0500–2400

EXTRA . . . EXTRA . . . At Waterloo Place, SW1, near St James's Park, is one of London's most spectacular monuments – the Duke of York's Column.

ST MARY ALDERMANBURY SQUARE,
Love Lane, EC2

A favourite lunchtime retreat, this small square lies on the site of St Mary Aldermanbury Church, which dates back to 1181. It was restored after the Great Fire of 1666 by Christopher Wren, but then gutted again during World War II. The park still retains the layout of the church. It is also the burial ground of Henry Condell and John Heminge, editors of the 1623 folio of Shakespeare's works, and a statue has been erected in their memory.

Tube: Bank, St Paul's, Moorgate
Open: all the time

EXTRA . . . EXTRA . . . The ruins of St Mary Aldermanbury Church were taken to Westminster College, Fulton,

Missouri, USA, in 1966 as a memorial to Winston Churchill.

TRENT PARK, Cockfosters, Barnet, Herts

Covering over 400 acres, this country park, once the seat of Sir Richard Jebb, physician to George III, was opened to the public in 1968. With ramblers, golfers, fishermen and horseriders all making the most of the facilities, there's plenty to watch. If you're feeling active, then wander through the park following one of the trails, or walk through the woodland spotting the wildlife on the way. There's also a 150-acre working farm, 'Fernyhill Farm', to explore. Take a picnic and enjoy the magnificent views.

Tube: Oakwood, Cockfosters
Open: all the time

EXTRA . . . EXTRA . . . Starting at the entrance opposite Cockfosters tube station, there's a Woodland Trail for blind people. This ¾-mile circuit, with messages in braille along the route, is designed so that blind people can enjoy the park on their own.

VICTORIA EMBANKMENT GARDENS,
Victoria Embankment, SW1, WC2 (*see also Walk 3, page 247*)

These gardens, divided by Northumberland Avenue, on the north bank of the Thames, are superbly kept and just the place for a few minutes' peace. There's also plenty to catch your eye as you walk through, with many statues, fountains, a lily pond, and a bandstand for summer concerts.

Tube: Embankment
Open: daily

EXTRA . . . EXTRA . . . The Embankment was built by Sir Joseph Bazalgette and completed in 1870. It is dedicated to Queen Victoria.

VICTORIA TOWER GARDENS, Millbank, SW1

These quiet gardens, although rather overshadowed by the Palace of Westminster, are a godsend for tired feet. You can sit on one of the benches overlooking the Thames and recover lost energy. There's usually a game of five-a-side football going on, and don't miss the statue of Emmeline Pankhurst, the famous suffragette.

Tube: Westminster
Open: daily

EXTRA . . . EXTRA . . . A short walk away is Smith Square, in its centre the 18th-century church of St John's, now a popular concert hall. Designed by Thomas Archer, the building was graphically described by Dickens as '. . . resembling some petrified monster, frightful and gigantic, on its back with its legs in the air'.

WANDSWORTH COMMON, Trinity Road, SW18

Sliced in two by a busy railway line, Wandsworth Common is definitely an urban open space. Yet it is surprisingly pretty, and very popular with local people. Here you can watch a game of tennis or bowls, walk a dog or have a pleasant picnic. But if you're keen on fitness training, take your sports clothes and prepare yourself for exercise. The fitness circuit is open for anyone who wants to have a go and it's lots of fun. A whole series of exercise 'equipment' is arranged around a large pitch: ladder walk, step-ups, hurdles, parallel bars, sit-up planks and, most daunting of all, a pole climb.

British Rail: Wandsworth Common
Open: all the time

EXTRA . . . EXTRA . . . The series of five roads between Trinity Road and Baskerville Road is described by local estate agents as 'the toast rack'!

WATERLOW PARK, Highgate High Street, N6 (*see also Walk 6, page 257*)

Although this pleasant park is, in fact, called after Sir Sydney Waterlow (Lord Mayor of London 1872–3), it could have derived its name from the vast expanses of water you see everywhere. It's the ponds with the water-fowl that really make it so attractive. There's also an aviary with a talkative mynah bird. Just inside the entrance to the 26-acre park is Lauderdale House, once the home of Nell Gwyn, and last lived in by Sir Sydney

Waterlow. There's a fine statue of Sir Sydney in the park, erected with money collected mainly by the poor of the district who recognized his virtues and good works.

Tube: Archway
Open: daily

EXTRA . . . EXTRA . . . Among the many notables who lived and worked in Highgate Village was the English poet and critic Samuel Taylor Coleridge, who lived and died at 3 The Grove, N6. Andrew Marvell, poet and assistant to John Milton, lived in a cottage in Highgate High Street which used to stand on the site of the entrance to Waterlow Park.

WESTMINSTER ABBEY GARDENS,

Westminster Abbey, Westminster, SW1 (*see also Walk 4, page 251*). Tel: 01-222 5152

It's rather like searching for the Secret Garden as you walk through the cloisters to find the College Garden at Westminster Abbey. And you certainly won't be disappointed. This land has been cultivated for 900 years – quite remarkable when you consider its situation right in the heart of London. As you enter the garden look to your right and you'll see the recently planted monastic herb garden, a replica of how it would have been in past centuries. There's also a colourful rose garden. (*See also Westminster Abbey, page 70.*)

Tube: Westminster, St James's Park
Open: Thursdays only, April–September, 1000–1800
October–March, 1000–1600

EXTRA . . . EXTRA . . . During August and early September there are band concerts in the gardens at lunchtimes between 1230 and 1400 on Thursdays.

WIMBLEDON COMMON, SW19. Tel: 01-788 7655

This large common (1,100 acres) is still relatively wild, though there are large open tracks which are popular with people walking their dogs. The common includes a golf course, which looks as though it has been 'shaved' out of the rough grassland. Look out for the 19th-century windmill – it's picturesque, but there is a charge to go inside.

British Rail: Wimbledon, then bus 80, 93
Tube: Putney Bridge, then bus 80, 93
Open: all the time

EXTRA . . . EXTRA . . . George Eliot (1819–80) lived in Wimbledon; she wrote *Mill on the Floss* while living at 31 Wimbledon Park Road, SW18.

CHAPTER SIX
People at Work

ARSENAL STADIUM, Avenell Road, Highbury, N5.
Tel: 226 0304

Here's your chance to take a behind-the-scenes look at one of London's top football clubs. The Royal Arsenal Football Club, or 'The Gunners' as they're better known, was founded in 1886 by workers at the Royal Armaments Factory in Woolwich and throughout the club there are pictures, mementos and trophies tracing its history right up to the present day – you could even meet some of the players! To see the club you must take a guided tour which lasts about an hour and a half and takes you around the boardroom, reception rooms, dressing rooms and outside to the pitch and stadium. The guide is so full of enthusiasm and fascinating titbits that a visit is always a real pleasure whether you're a football fan or not.

Tube: Arsenal
Open: Tours start at 1030 Monday–Friday on days when the stadium is not in use. Apply first in writing to Guided Tours, Arsenal Stadium, Avenell Road, London N5 giving preferred dates.

EXTRA . . . EXTRA . . . Arsenal underground station is the only one in London to take its name from a football club.

AUCTIONS

Going, going . . . make sure that you don't nod your head and find that pricey antique has 'gone' in your direction. Auction houses can be really exciting places to visit with thousands of pounds changing hands between dealers and experts. But you'll also find amateurs there too and you can often pick up a good bargain. The items up for auction vary according to the house and the day, so it's best to check before going:

Bonhams, Montpelier Galleries, Montpelier Street, SW7. Tel: 01-584 9161. **Tube:** Knightsbridge
Christie's, 85 Old Brompton Road, SW7.
Tel: 01-581 2231. **Tube:** South Kensington
Greasby's, 211 Longley Road, SW17. Tel: 01-672 1100.
Tube: Tooting Broadway
Harvey's Auctions, Neal Street, WC2. Tel: 01-240 1464.
Tube: Covent Garden
Phillips, Blenstock House, 7 Blenheim Street, New Bond Street, W1. Tel: 01-629 6602. **Tube:** Bond Street
Sotheby's, 34–35 New Bond Street, W1. Tel: 01-493 8080. **Tube:** Bond Street

---

EXTRA . . . EXTRA . . . Most of the auction houses are happy to value your antiques or bric-à-brac free of charge (ask in advance) – so here's the place to find out how much that family heirloom is worth.

BILLINGSGATE, North Quay, West India Dock Road, Isle of Dogs, E14

Porters in this huge fish market can sometimes still be spotted wearing traditional leather and wood hats on which they balance heavy boxes of fish. The wet fish – there's a wide variety – and the damp floor both shine as water seems to drip from everything. Do keep out of the way of the very busy traders.

Tube: Mile End, then bus 277
Bus: 56, 277, N84, N85
Open: Tuesday–Saturday, 0300–0900

EXTRA . . . EXTRA . . . The present Billingsgate market was opened in 1982 when it was moved from its old site in EC3. It was named after a river gate in the City wall. The wharf is perhaps the oldest on the Thames – in use since Saxon times.

BOROUGH MARKET, Cathedral Street, SE1

The best time to arrive at this wholesale fruit, vegetable and flower market is at 0530 when the trading begins. Although smaller than Spitalfields Market (*page 194*), it is renowned for its high-quality goods and friendly atmosphere, and you can't help but sense the great pride felt by the stall-holders who have worked here for generations. The market seems to be well organized and the produce is carefully laid out. Stay well in the background and just watch the experts at work.

The market used to be held on London Bridge in the

13th century and moved to its present site in the shadows of Southwark Cathedral (*page 66*) in 1756. It forms a triangle to the west of Borough High Street between Winchester Walk, Storey Street and Bedale Street.

Tube: London Bridge
Bus: Night bus N89
Open: Monday–Saturday, 0230–1100

EXTRA . . . EXTRA . . . Until 1750 London Bridge was the only bridge across the Thames, and so many of the main roads passed through here. Hence the huge number of inns in the area. Look at the street names for a clue to past inns – King's Head Yard, White Hart Yard. Many 17th-century inns still exist, but the one to look for in particular is The George Inn in Borough High Street, now owned by the National Trust. This is the last surviving galleried inn in London, and its façade dates back to 1676. Incidentally, several pubs near Borough Market open at 0630 for traders. In Dickens's *Pickwick Papers*, Sam Weller is said to have had an early lunch at one of these, 'two or three pounds of cold beef and a pot or two of porter after the fatigues of Borough Market'.

CENTRAL CRIMINAL COURT, Old Bailey, Newgate Street, EC4. Tel: 01-248 3277

Don't be surprised to find a group of journalists and photographers standing outside. The 'Old Bailey', as these courts are known, are where all the principal criminal cases in the country are tried and there's usually something newsworthy going on. You probably won't get a place to watch the proceedings in Court 1, but there are often interesting cases in the other 18 courts. You're welcome to sit in the Public Galleries while the courts are in session. The attendants will give you a rundown of the day's cases, but it's very much pot luck and unfortunately some trials can be rather drawn-out and dull. But take a good look around and take it all in – the Judge, the Officers of Court, the barristers, and the secretary whose shorthand is so fast you can hardly see the pen move. No cameras or tape recorders are allowed in.

The 'Old Bailey' stands on the site of Newgate Prison, notorious for its appalling conditions and lack of justice. From 1783 until its abolition in 1868, this was the place for public executions. The building is surmounted by a 12-foot-tall statue of the Lady of Justice, balancing scales in an outstretched hand. To visit you must be over 14. (*See also Royal Courts of Justice, page 191.*)

Tube: St Paul's, Chancery Lane
Open: Monday–Friday, 1030–1300, 1400–1600

EXTRA . . . EXTRA . . . Walk to the junction of Giltspur Street, EC1, and Cock Lane, EC1, and you'll see the statue of a rather tubby little boy. There used to be an inscription beneath: 'This boy is in memory put up of the late Fire of London, occasioned by the sin of gluttony 1666.' This site used to be known as Pie Corner – and so the saying that the Fire began in Pudding Lane and ended at Pie Corner.

COURT OF COMMON COUNCIL, Guildhall Yard, EC2

All London's boroughs have council meetings which are open to the public and which can be extremely entertaining, but the most interesting council meeting is perhaps that of the Court of Common Council. The meeting, which evolved in the 13th century, is attended by the Lord Mayor who is accompanied by the City Marshal, the Swordbearer and the Macebearer. The last three proceed into the Guildhall (*page 42*) at a measured pace which fascinates visitors, but gets barely a glance from office workers. In the Swordbearer's fur head-dress is a hidden pocket which holds the Lord Mayor's key to the City Seal Box. There are free agendas on each seat to tell you what's going on.

Tube: Bank, Moorgate, St Paul's
Open: Thursdays, roughly every three weeks;
  tel: 01-606 3030 for a specific date
Time: 1300 (lasting one–two hours)

EXTRA . . . EXTRA . . . As you walk round the City don't forget to use your nose; interesting smells (mainly nice ones!) waft up from hidden cellar restaurants and bars.

FORD MOTOR COMPANY, Dagenham Plant, Dagenham, Essex. Tel: 01-592 3000

It takes 22½ working days to make one car so don't expect to see the whole process, but a visit to the Ford

Motor Company gives a marvellous insight into the many processes involved and a reassuring look at the stringent safety tests and checks. It would be much too dangerous to let people wander at will, so you're guided around by an expert who will help explain the various techniques, introduce you to the friendly robots and, when the noise level permits, answer all your questions. The Ford estate at Dagenham is huge – covering almost 1.7 square miles, and the tour, which lasts nearly two hours, is quite demanding because of the distance you walk (around two miles!) and the facts you absorb, but don't worry, there's tea and biscuits halfway through to keep up your energy level! No individual bookings are taken but family outings are encouraged, or why not get together with a group of friends?

British Rail: Dagenham Dock
Tube: Dagenham Heathway, then bus 174 or 175
Open: Tours take place Monday–Friday (except plant holidays) 0945–1330. To book telephone Factory Tours Office 01-592 3000 giving preferred dates. Minimum age is 10 years.

EXTRA . . . EXTRA . . . The first vehicle to be built at the Dagenham Plant was a Model AA truck. It left the production line at exactly 0115 on 1 October 1931.

THE GLASSHOUSE, 65 Long Acre, London WC2. Tel: 01-836 9785

Everyone is welcome to watch the craftsmen here. There's a special viewing gallery, so you can see the huge furnaces and glass-blowing area. You're not near enough to ask for a running commentary, but you can easily pick up what they're doing. Unfortunately you can't watch them doing the cutting and finishing as the workshops are below the shop. Beautiful glass is on display in the front area, including work by Moore and Solven, who both worked at The Glasshouse.

Tube: Covent Garden
Open: Monday–Friday, 1000–1730 (no blowing
     1300–1400), Saturday, 1100–1630

EXTRA . . . EXTRA . . . Seven Dials, WC2, is just a few minutes' walk away. This is where seven streets meet. There used to be (and there are restoration plans afoot) a Doric column in the centre of the circus which was capped with seven sundials.

THE HOUSES OF PARLIAMENT, Palace of Westminster, SW1. Tel: 01-219 3000 (*see also Walk 4, page 251*)

Seats in the Strangers' Gallery of the Houses of Lords and Commons are limited, so to listen to debates and watch Parliament in action you have to join a rather slow-moving queue starting from St Stephen's Porch. But once inside you'll be treated with full pomp and ceremony as you are shown to your seat and handed a copy of the order of the day's business. To see more, and to get a good explanation of some of the rather complicated rituals and procedures, it's a good idea to write to your MP asking him to arrange a visit for you. If you're from overseas, then apply for a letter of introduction from your Embassy or High Commission. The Palace of Westminster, a Victorian Gothic building, was designed by Barry and Pugin and built between 1840 and 1868 on the site of the Old Palace of Westminster. (*See also State Opening, page 228.*)

Tube: Westminster
Open: Monday–Thursday, 1430 onwards, Friday, 1000 onwards

EXTRA . . . EXTRA . . . Walk along Whitehall to 10 Downing Street, SW1. This house, with its Georgian façade, has been the home of the Prime Minister since 1731 when Sir Robert Walpole lived here. It's interesting to note that the street was built and named after Sir George Downing, a diplomat, courtier – and rogue!

LLOYD'S OF LONDON, Lime Street, EC3.
Tel: 01-623 7100 ext. 6210

Right in the heart of the City of London, amidst some of its most conservative office complexes and adjacent to the attractive Victorian Leadenhall Market (*see page 85*), can be found the most uncompromising modern building in the capital – Lloyd's of London. The work of architect Richard Rogers, its glass, steel and concrete frame, with service towers and glazed exterior lifts, has many of the qualities of the greatest Victorian engineering; however, you must go inside to fully appreciate its outstanding design qualities. Visitors may not enter the working environment at Lloyd's, but a special high level viewing area has been provided. Reached by a lift which glides effortlessly up the building (offering unusual views down side streets) the visitors' area includes a small exhibition which outlines the activities of Lloyd's as the world's leading insurance market. But it's the memory of the spectacular, deep atrium which every visitor takes away with them. Floor after floor of busy brokers scuttling from desk to desk is revealed, while high above them, through the glass roof, can be seen the bright blue maintenance cranes which now form such a distinctive part of the City skyline.

Tube: Bank, Monument.
Open: Monday–Friday 1000–1430 (booked parties 1230–1545)

EXTRA . . . EXTRA . . . Lloyd's dates back almost three hundred years to a coffee house owned by Edward Lloyd. It became, like many other such establishments, a centre for discussion and gossip. Lloyd's, however, quickly gained a reputation for reliable shipping news and thus became a meeting place for people concerned with trade and commerce including merchants dealing in insurance policies.

THE LONDON GLASSBLOWING WORKSHOP, Hope (Sufferance) Wharf, 109 Rotherhithe Street, SE16. Tel: 01-237 0394

A visit to this well-established glassblowing studio – one of the first in Britain to specialize in designer-made blown glass – is split into two parts – gallery and workshop. First take a look at the gallery, simple but attractive, where beautiful pieces of glass are displayed to advantage; the iridescent colours are particularly surprising. Then cross the road and see how these exquisitely crafted works are made – it's an exciting process.

Tube: Rotherhithe
Open: Monday–Friday, 1100–1800

EXTRA . . . EXTRA . . . The London Glassblowing Workshop is tucked away behind perhaps the most beautiful church in this part of London – St Mary's. There's been a church on this spot for over 1,000 years, though the present one was completed in 1710. Inside there are many reminders of Rotherhithe's seafaring tradition. Look out for the plaque on the wall commemorating the burial (in 1622) of Captain Christopher Jones, Master of the *Mayflower* – it was from Rotherhithe that the *Mayflower* sailed for the New World.

LONDON SILVER VAULTS, Chancery Lane, WC2

This is a must for silver-lovers. The vaults comprise a basement full of shops selling a fine collection of silverware, both antique and modern. The traders, all devoted to silver, are quite happy to talk about their goods, look up hallmarks and explain the histories. You'll be amazed at some of the enormous sums asked for the tiniest items, and equally surprised at how many people are willing to pay. The vaults never seem to be over-crowded and the traders, who are understandably silver-snobs, like it that way. You'll want to go back again and again. (*See also Goldsmiths' Hall, page 41*.)

Tube: Chancery Lane
Open: Monday–Friday, 0900–1700, Saturday, 0900–1230

EXTRA . . . EXTRA . . . The Essex Head pub, now called 'Edgar Wallace', in Essex Street, WC2, was built in the 17th century. This is where Dr Johnson and his friends used to hold weekly discussion meetings.

MOUNT PLEASANT POST OFFICE,
Farringdon Road, EC1. Tel: 01-239 2191

Mount Pleasant is the largest sorting office in the world. It is open 24 hours a day and handles around three million letters each day. A visit is a pretty mind-boggling experience – you just won't believe the number and variety of cards, letters, parcels and packets, all sizes and colours with stamps from all over the world. You must take a guided tour, which lasts around two hours. You're taken around the Sorting Office, the Code Sort Area and finally shown the Post Office Railway. This railway system has no guards or drivers and carries no passengers but it runs for 22 hours a day, successfully carrying some 35,000 bags of mail to seven different points between Paddington and Whitechapel. You'll find it all fascinating especially as the guide is so keen to explain the different stages and help you understand the system.

Tube: Chancery Lane, Farringdon
Open: Tours Monday–Thursday at 1030, 1430 and 1930.

Telephone or write in advance to The Postmaster Controller (above address).

EXTRA . . . EXTRA . . . The name Mount Pleasant conjures up a delightful image but don't be misled. The 'Mount' is understandable as it's on a hill, but Pleasant? Apparently, this was ironic! It was once a dirty place, popular for dumping rubbish.

NEW COVENT GARDEN, Nine Elms Lane, SW8

Two wholesale markets at New Covent Garden Market are bustling with activity by 0600. The fruit and vegetable market is fast and furious – porters trundling the huge loads around are lethal! The flower market is more friendly, and a few brave shoppers can be spotted buying single bunches (though this is definitely not encouraged). This indoor market is kept at a constant warm temperature that seems to bring out the scents of the flowers which mingle to make a heady perfume. The vegetable market is rather more chilly but a warming cup of tea and perhaps a sandwich can be bought to keep out the cold from tea trolleys inside both markets.

Tube: Vauxhall
Bus: 77 and 77A
Open: Flower market, Monday–Friday, 0400–1100 (go as early as you can), Saturday, 0400–0900. Fruit and vegetable market, Monday–Friday, 0400–1200

EXTRA . . . EXTRA . . . It is interesting to note that the name Vauxhall comes from 'the manor belonging to

Falkes' – Faukeshale. Falkes was a supporter of King John and documentation of the name dates back to 1279.

THE ROYAL BRITISH LEGION POPPY FACTORY, 20 Petersham Road, Richmond, Surrey. Tel: 01-940 3305

Believe it or not, around 45 million poppies, 180,000 remembrance crosses, and about 65,000 wreaths are made here every year. The workers are all disabled exservicemen and women who are happy to tell you all about how the poppies, wreaths and crosses are put together – and it's not as easy as you might think! Tours last an hour and a half (and that includes a free cup of tea!) and you're shown all areas of the factory and given a full explanation of the story behind the poppy as the symbol of remembrance. The tours are popular so do book well in advance. (*See also Remembrance Sunday, page 233.*)

Tube: Richmond
Note: to book a tour contact The Manager at the above
          address.

EXTRA . . . EXTRA . . . The poppy was first described as the 'Flower of Remembrance' by Colonel John McCrae in a poem written in pencil on a page torn from his despatch book during the second battle of Ypres in 1915.

ROYAL COURTS OF JUSTICE, Strand, WC2.
Tel: 01-936 6000

All the main civil cases in the country are brought to trial
in this huge Gothic building known as 'The Law Courts'.
Designed by G. E. Street, it was built in 1874–82, and
even if you don't want to visit a court the main hall is still
worth a visit. Experience the feeling of space and history
as you walk across the vast mosaic floor. The court cases
tend to be less interesting than at the 'Old Bailey' (*see
page 180*), but it's still good to see justice in action.

There's an exhibition of legal costumes, maces and
scrolls from home and abroad, dating back to the early
19th century. Here you can see the amazing full-bottomed
wig of powdered horsehair worn by Clement Tudway
Swanston, QC, in the mid-19th century.

Tube: Temple
Open: Monday–Friday, 1000-1600

EXTRA . . . EXTRA . . . Opposite the Royal Courts of
Justice is Twining's shop, famed world-wide for its tea.
This was the original 'Tom's Coffee House', bought by
Thomas Twining in 1706. He soon realized that competition among coffee houses in the area was great and started
selling tea instead. Business boomed and among the
famous tea-drinkers to be found in the café was Dr
Samuel Johnson. Note the golden lion above the doorway. This was a means of identification as there were no
street numbers at the time.

ST KATHARINE DOCK

Although St Katharine Dock has now become a major tourist attraction with The Tower Hotel, Dickens' Inn and the Beefeater-by-the-Tower-Restaurant, famed for its medieval banquets, all catering for visitors, it's important to remember that the docks are also a commercial centre. In its heyday, this was a real treasure-store dealing with shiploads of ivory, silver and spices from all over the world. However, the docks were forced to close down after World War II and it wasn't until the 1960s that reconstruction started.

With the opening of the World Trade Centre here in 1972, it became a centre for international business. The docks are in action again as well, with about 200 moorings of private craft. It's a lovely place to wander around, day or night, with plenty to see and do. But it's best to avoid buying anything from the rather over-priced shops or restaurants and bars. Instead, soak up the atmosphere of old combined with new. You can pick up a free leaflet all about St Katharine Dock at Tourist Information Centres.

Tube: Tower Hill

EXTRA . . . EXTRA . . . Cross over Tower Bridge, turn right along the river bank, and you'll get a good view of HMS *Belfast*, once the flagship of the British Fleet in the Far East and the last surviving big-gun ship of the Royal Navy. She is moored at Symon's Wharf, Vine Lane, SE1. Enjoy the view for free, but if you want to look around inside then you have to pay.

SMITHFIELD, EC1

This wholesale meat market is one of the oldest and largest in Europe. Vans start arriving at midnight when porters, with their blood-stained white overalls, begin to unload the carcasses. Then the weighing, marking and displaying begins, ready for business at 0500. It's very much a working market with lorryloads of meat changing hands rather than individual joints. It's certainly not the place to go if you don't like the sight of blood, as everywhere you look are carcasses and bins full of hearts, livers and other 'bits'.

The site was once a 'smoothfield', and from the 14th century was used as a cattle market and site for archery competitions and fayres.

Tube: Farringdon, Barbican
Open: Monday–Friday, 0500–0900

EXTRA . . . EXTRA . . . A part of Smithfield used to be known as The Elms, and this was where, until the mid-14th century, public executions took place. It's also interesting to note that in the reign of Queen Mary (1553–8) it's estimated that about 280 people were burned to death in England for heresy. And it was at Smithfield that most of them died.

SOUTH BANK CRAFTS CENTRE, Hungerford Arches, South Bank, SE1. Tel: 01-928 0681

Squeezed into a small space beside the Royal Festival Hall (*see page 26*), the South Bank Crafts Centre is easy

to overlook. But this workshop for some 14 craftspeople
is worth seeking out as visitors can see a variety of crafts
being practised and ask about methods of production – as
well as admire the finished items on display in the centre's
shop! Crafts represented include: jewellery making in
precious and non-precious materials; fabric printing; felt
production for use in wall hangings and rugs; knitting;
weaving; embroidery; ceramics and pottery.

Tube: Waterloo
Open: Tuesday–Sunday, 1100–1930

EXTRA . . . EXTRA . . . There are regular crafts events
at the Royal Festival Hall and you can see a craft
showcase on level 2.

SPITALFIELDS, E1

The first thing you notice about this wholesale fruit,
vegetable and flower market is its sheer size. Indeed, the
market, which lies on the west side of Commercial Street,
covers twelve acres in all. The quantity of produce changing hands is also vast, with about 1500 tons of fruit and
vegetables sold each day. There's also a flower market
nestling between Lamb Street and Folgate Street. Keep
your eyes alert if you're visiting Spitalfields, as lorries and
fork-lift trucks seem to come at you from all directions.

Trading usually begins at 0430, and by noon the area
has changed from a lively hubbub of business to a rather
bleak and tatty yard with a few squashed tomatoes and
apples lying in the gutters.

Tube: Liverpool Street
Open: Monday–Friday, 0430–1100
　　　　Saturday, 0430–0900

EXTRA . . . EXTRA . . . The gardens of Christ Church, Spitalfields, in Commercial Street, E1, are known as 'Itchy Park' by East Enders. This dates back to the days when the benches were a favourite haunt of London's down-and-outs. They were always itching! But don't be put off. They're now very pleasant gardens for a quiet sit with an adventure playground for children at the back.

STEPPING STONES FARM, Stepney Way, E1.
Tel: 01-790 8204

You might not expect to see a working farm in London but here it is! You can see sheep, goats, ducks, donkeys, pigs and ponies in this 4-acre plot. The staff are friendly and enthusiastic and will tell you all about everyday life on a city farm. This is just one of the growing number of City Farms, set up in major cities to show residents what life on a farm is really like. For a full list contact the National Federation of City Farms, The Old Vicarage, 66 Frazer Street, Windmill Hill, Bedminster, Bristol BS3 4LY (please enclose a sae). Although your visit to Stepping Stones is free, the animals do like something to eat – preferably fruit or vegetable peelings.

Tube: Vauxhall
Open: daily, 1030–1700

EXTRA . . . EXTRA . . . Back in the 16th century and before, much of London was farmland. You only have to look at the number of streets called Farm Road, Farm Lane, Farmlands and other variations to be reminded that London wasn't always a built-up city.

CHAPTER SEVEN
Annual Events

CHARLES I COMMEMORATION, Whitehall, SW1

On 30 January 1649, Charles I was taken from the Banqueting House, Whitehall, to his death at the scaffold. To commemorate this event members of the Kings Army, dressed and armed in 17th-century style, march from St James's Palace. Following the route of Charles' last walk they proceed along The Mall to Banqueting House where a wreath is laid and a short service held before continuing to Charles' statue in Trafalgar Square and then back to St James's Palace.

Tube: Charing Cross
Date: last Sunday in January
Time: Tel: 01-730 3488 (London Tourist Board and Convention Bureau)

EXTRA . . . EXTRA . . . When he reached the scaffold, Charles I's last words were, 'I go from a corruptible to an incorruptible crown.'

CHINESE NEW YEAR, Soho, W1

New Year is the high spot of the Chinese calendar. Soho comes alive with decorations: streamers and garlands hanging from windows and balconies. The atmosphere is electric, with music and colourfully costumed dancers. Large crowds gather to see the famous 'Lion Dance' – young men dressed in a brightly decorated lion costume weave their way through the streets and are given gifts of money and food along the route.

Tube: Tottenham Court Road, Piccadilly Circus
Date: the date is based on cycles of the moon and the sun and thus it changes every year. The festivities take place on the nearest Sunday to the date of the Chinese New Year.
Time: Tel: 01-730 3488 (London Tourist Board and Convention Bureau)

EXTRA ... EXTRA ... There's an interesting tale attached to the name Soho. Hard as it is to imagine when looking at seedy, built-up, present-day Soho, the area was once open fields popular for hunting. Cries of 'so-so', the French equivalent of 'tally-ho', were often heard, hence the label Soho which has ever since been associated with this part of London.

BLESSING THE THROATS, Church of St Etheldreda, Ely Place, EC1

This unusual sounding ceremony commemorates St Blaise, Patron Saint of those suffering from throat infections. On the feast-day of St Blaise a Roman Catholic priest blesses anyone with a throat infection. (*See also St Etheldreda's, page 55.*)

Tube: Chancery Lane, Farringdon
Date: 3 February
Time: frequent intervals throughout the day

EXTRA . . . EXTRA . . . St Blaise was martyred in A.D. 316. Legend has it that he miraculously cured a boy who was dying because of a fish-bone stuck in his throat.

CLOWN SERVICE, Holy Trinity Church,
Beechwood Road, Dalston, E8

Members of Clowns International Club, in full costume, gather for a special service at Holy Trinity Church. During the service a wreath is laid on the memorial to Grimaldi – who originated the clown character and costume we recognize still. After the ceremony a free clown show is given in the church hall – children love it!

British Rail: Dalston Junction
Bus: 30, 38
Date: first Sunday in February
Time: Tel: 01-730 3488 (London Tourist Board and
          Convention Bureau)

EXTRA . . . EXTRA . . . The costume Grimaldi created is now preserved in the Museum of London, London Wall, EC2 (*see page 121*).

PANCAKE DAY, Lincoln's Inn Fields, WC2

Pancake Day is now an annual event. It traditionally marks the beginning of Lent when fat and meat were forbidden and so were used up in savoury pancakes. The art of 'tossing the pancake' has now become something of a sport and races are held throughout the country. In London, Lincoln's Inn Fields is taken over by housewives, chefs, personalities and beauty queens who run a 100-yard course tossing their pancakes three times. (*See also Lincoln's Inn Fields, page 163.*)

Tube: Holborn
Date: Shrove Tuesday
Time: races begin 1100

EXTRA . . . EXTRA . . . Lincoln's Inn is one of the four great Inns of Court and the custom of ringing a curfew bell has survived here.

SIR JOHN CASS, RED FEATHER DAY, Church of St Botolph, Aldgate High Street, EC3

Pupils and staff from the Sir John Cass School attend a memorial service to their founder, each wearing a scarlet feather. The plume signifies the quill used by Sir John Cass who, tradition has it, while signing his will leaving money to maintain the school, died from a haemorrhage – blood is said to have stained his pen. After the service staff and guests drink a toast in hot mulled wine.

Tube: Aldgate
Date: on or near 20 February

Time: Tel: 01-730 3488 (London Tourist Board and
Convention Bureau)

EXTRA . . . EXTRA . . . There is a mummified head in
the church which is said to be that of Lady Jane Grey's
father.

BRIDEWELL SERVICE, St Bride's Church, Fleet
Street, EC1

Bridewell Royal Hospital was founded in 1553 by King
Edward VI as a shelter for homeless men and women of
the City; a place where they could learn a trade such as
spinning or weaving. However, things did not quite go
according to plan and when a prison was opened next
door many problems arose. Eventually the shelter was
closed and instead a 'House of Occupation' was established. This institution was later moved to Witley in
Surrey. A service of Dedication and Thanksgiving is held
each year and is attended by the Lord Mayor and/or
Sheriffs and the pupils and staff of the King Edward VI
School, Witley. (*See also St Bride's Church, page 55*).

Tube: Aldwych
Date: second Tuesday in March
Time: 1200

EXTRA . . . EXTRA . . . Walk down to Fleet Street,
EC4. and you'll see a memorial to mark the Temple Bar.
This Bar was set up in the Middle Ages as the western
entrance to the City of London. In its place now stands a
memorial pillar with a statue of Queen Victoria and the

future Edward VII which is capped with the unofficial badge of the City, a griffin. This is still where the Sovereign stops when she visits the City to be met by the Lord Mayor and receive the Pearl Sword.

DRUID SOLSTICE

Each spring and autumn the Order of Druids celebrate, with ancient ritual, the seasons of renewal (spring) and of harvest (autumn).

The Spring Equinox ceremony is held on Tower Hill Terrace, EC3.

Tube: Tower Hill
Date: March

The Autumn Equinox ceremony is held on Primrose Hill, Regent's Park, NW3.

Tube: Camden Town
Date: September
Contact the London Tourist Board and Convention Bureau for more information. Tel: 01-730 3488

EXTRA ... EXTRA ... The Druids' costume has not changed since the 18th century when interest in this very old Order was revived. However, the ancient Druids probably went naked!

ORANGES AND LEMONS SERVICE, Church of St Clement Danes, Strand, WC2

Children of St Clement Danes School have their own 'oranges and lemons' service after which they are each given an orange and a lemon to celebrate the day when oranges and lemons first arrived in London.

Tube: Aldwych
Date: March
Time: Tel: 01-730 3488 (London Tourist Board and Convention Bureau)

EXTRA . . . EXTRA . . . In 1920 the vicar of St Clement Danes installed bells which could ring out the tune of the old nursery rhyme which goes 'Oranges and lemons say the bells of St Clements . . .'

BOAT RACE, Thames (Putney–Mortlake)

This very competitive race between the first eights of Oxford and Cambridge universities has been waged for over 150 years. It takes place between Putney and Mortlake, and large crowds gather on the banks of the Thames to cheer on the competitors while a flotilla of small boats bobs alongside. The course is 4 miles 374 yards from start to finish.

Tube: Putney Bridge
Date: March or April: tel: 01-730 3488 (London Tourist Board and Convention Bureau)
Time: starting times vary according to the tide

EXTRA . . . EXTRA . . . Thamesday, held each summer on and beside the river, is a spectacular day out. Celebrations include a naval display, powerboat and canoe races, fairs and fireworks. To find out the date contact the London Tourist Board and Convention Bureau, tel: 01-730 3488.

BUTTERWORTH CHARITY, St Bartholomew-the-Great, Smithfield, EC1

During the 17th century hot-cross buns and coins were laid on the tombstones of St Bartholomew-the-Great (*page 54*) for the 'poor widows of the parish'. However, there is now a shortage of 'poor widows' so the custom has been altered slightly and the buns are given to children.

Tube: St Paul's, Farringdon, Barbican
Date: Good Friday
Time: 1100

EXTRA . . . EXTRA . . . This distribution of sticky buns in perpetuity was ensured during the 19th century by Joshua Butterworth – hence the name Butterworth Charity.

EASTER PARADE, Battersea Park, SW11

An excellent day out for all the family. There are side-shows and stalls all day, but the real climax is the Easter Parade. Huge crowds line the mile-long route taken by the procession round the perimeter of the park – so get there early for a good view of the brightly coloured floats and bands.

Bus: 137
Date: Easter Sunday
Time: the parade begins at 1500

EXTRA . . . EXTRA . . . Battersea Park (*see page 144*) now covers nearly 200 acres, but before its establishment as a park it was a very lonely area used for duels. One of the last fights was between Lord Winchelsea and the Duke of Wellington.

HANGING THE BUN, The Widow's Son, 75 Devons Road, Bow, E3

Each year a sailor puts a new bun with the collection of old ones, black with age, which hang over the bar of The Widow's Son. Two hundred years ago on the site of this pub was the cottage home of a widow whose only son was a sailor. Expecting him home for Easter she baked a hot-cross bun for him. He did not return and she never heard from him again, but each year she baked another bun. When she died the collected buns were found hanging from a beam in her cottage, which became known as 'Bun House'.

British Rail: Bromley-by-Bow
Tube: Bow Road, then bus 10, 25
Bus: 25
Date: Good Friday
Time: Tel: 01-730 3488 (London Tourist Board and
        Convention Bureau)

EXTRA . . . EXTRA . . . Occasionally, extra buns have
been added to the collection to mark a special event; for
example, the coronation of Elizabeth II in 1953.

HARNESS HORSE PARADE, Inner Circle,
Regent's Park, NW1

A rally of working horses, traditional brewers' drays, carts
and carriages tours Regent's Park (*page 165*) competing
for rosettes. A fine sight which gives some idea of London
life before the invention of the car.

Tube: Regent's Park, Great Portland Street
Date: Easter Monday
Time: 0930 veterinary inspection. Grand parade of
        winners 1200

EXTRA . . . EXTRA . . . In Hanover Lodge on the Outer
Circle of Regent's Park, Joseph Bonaparte, Napoleon's
brother, lived in exile.

MAUNDY MONEY

Each year on Maundy Thursday the Queen distributes specially minted coins, a custom which dates back to at least the 12th century. Originally the coins were given to poor people, but now they are given to orphans or children of widows, and to people who have given service to the church.

Distribution is from a different church each year; contact the London Tourist Board and Convention Bureau, tel: 01-730 3488, for venue and time.

EXTRA ... EXTRA ... In the original ceremony the monarch first washed then kissed the feet of the poor. This rite was stopped by Charles I at the outbreak of the plague. The custom was revived by Charles II and perpetuated by James II and William III, the last monarch to carry out the full ritual.

TYBURN WALK

In silence, a procession of two or three thousand people, led by a Catholic Bishop, walk from the Old Bailey (*see page 180*) to Tyburn Convent (Bayswater Road) in memory of Catholics martyred at Tyburn gallows during the 16th and 17th centuries.

Tube: St Paul's, Marble Arch
Date: last Sunday in April
Time: Tel: 01-730 3488 (London Tourist Board and Convention Bureau)

EXTRA . . . EXTRA . . . The gallows at Tyburn were last used in 1783, when John Austin was hanged. The gallows were a triangular shape 12 feet high, and up to 8 people could be hanged on each of its three sides.

LONDON MARATHON, Greenwich Park, SE3, to Westminster Bridge, SW1

Up to 20,000 runners of all shapes and sizes test their stamina over this gruelling 26 mile, 385 yard course through the streets and over the bridges of London. They come from all over the world – athletes, celebrities and charity fund-raisers dressed in fancy costumes. There's a special race for wheelchair athletes which starts on Blackheath at about 0925, followed by the main race which begins at 0930. The leaders usually cross the finishing line on Westminster Bridge at about 1140. The rest? Wait and see! For some runners it's a serious challenge, for others it's a fun day out, but for everyone it's a sporting spectacle enjoyed by participants and spectators alike. (*See also Greenwich Park, page 154.*)

Tube: Start: New Cross, New Cross Gate, then bus 53
       Finish: Westminster
Date: late April, for specific date tel: 01-730 3488
       (London Tourist Board and Convention Bureau)

EXTRA . . . EXTRA . . . Another popular running event is the London to Brighton Running Race held in October each year. For details tel: 01-393 8950.

SPITAL SERMON, St Lawrence Jewry-next-Guildhall, Gresham Street, EC2

This sermon is well worth going to see as it's attended by the Lord Mayor, Sheriffs and Aldermen of the City. They parade in a colourful procession across Guildhall yard for a service and sermon in the church of St Lawrence Jewry-next-Guildhall (*page 58*). It's held annually to bring together all the staff of the City's two great hospitals – Christ's Hospital and the Bridewell – to reconfirm the City's historic commitment to both establishments. (*See also Guildhall, page 42.*)

Tube: St Paul's
Date: 2nd Wednesday after Easter
Time: Tel: 01-730 3488 (London Tourist Board and Convention Bureau)

EXTRA . . . EXTRA . . . The Spital Sermon used to be extremely long. The record is for the sermon preached by a Dr Barrow who spoke for 3½ hours to his congregation – who were standing!

FLORENCE NIGHTINGALE COMMEMORATION SERVICE, Westminster Abbey, Parliament Square, SW1

Florence Nightingale left England in 1854 with a team of 37 nurses to help soldiers in Scutari, where the legend of her as the 'lady with the lamp' grew. The commemoration service in the Abbey begins with a procession of Chelsea Pensioners who represent the soldiers she cared for.

During the service a lamp is carried from St George's Chapel to the Sanctuary and is placed on the High Altar. (*See also Westminster Abbey, page 70.*)

Tube: Westminster
Date: on or near 12 May
Time: Tel: 01-730 3488 (London Tourist Board and Convention Bureau)

EXTRA . . . EXTRA . . . At the foot of Lower Regent Street is 'Guards Monument', a memorial to the 22,162 guardsmen who died in the Crimean War. To the right is a statue of Florence Nightingale.

LONDON TO BRIGHTON BIKE RACE, Hyde Park, W1

Literally thousands of bicycles of all shapes and sizes – with one wheel, two, or three and even four – gather in Hyde Park (*page 158*) for this increasingly popular event. All ages take part, for this isn't a race (except in the eyes of the really keen cyclists at the front) – it's more like a family outing. The route out of London is temporarily a no-go area for motorized vehicles, as pedal-pushers flood out of the gates of Hyde Park at the start of their long journey to Brighton. (*See also the London to Brighton Veteran Car Run, page 231.*)

Tube: Hyde Park Corner
Date: May

EXTRA . . . EXTRA . . . Why not take part in the race? It's free, all you need is a bike! For details, Tel: 01-

730 3488 (London Tourist Board and Convention Bureau).

BEATING THE BOUNDS, All Hallows-by-the-Tower, EC3

During the Middle Ages there were very few maps, so to establish parish boundaries a custom of Beating the Bounds developed. Nowadays, each year in May or June, a procession round boundary marks takes place. The parish marks include one in the middle of the Thames so a Port of London boat takes members of the procession to the mark; a choir boy is then held by the ankles while he 'whacks' the boundary over the side of the boat! (*See also All Hallows-by-the-Tower, page 33.*)

Tube: Tower Hill
Date: May or June
Time: Tel: 01-730 3488 (London Tourist Board and
Convention Bureau)

EXTRA . . . EXTRA . . . If you're near the Thames to see the 'whacking', look out for the Mute Swan. It has been regarded as a royal bird for as long as records exist.

BUBBLE SERMON, St Martin-within-Ludgate, Ludgate Hill, EC4

Richard Johnson (a grammarian, and member of the Stationers' Company) left in his will money to be given to the poor members of the Stationers' Company and for an annual sermon entitled 'Bulla est vita humana', which means 'Life is a Bubble'. The Company gathers each year to listen to the sermon and to honour their benefactor.

Tube: St Pauls, Blackfriars
Date: 1st Tuesday in June
Time: Tel: 01-730 3488 (London Tourist Board and Convention Bureau)

EXTRA . . . EXTRA . . . St Martin-within-Ludgate is on the south side of the Garden Court of Stationers' Hall. This is where heretical books used to be burned and it's said that the trees in the Garden Court grow in the ashes of these books. Approach the court via Stationers' Hall Court, EC4, off Ludgate Hill.

SAMUEL PEPYS COMMEMORATION SERVICE, St Olave, Hart Street, EC3

Samuel Pepys, in his vivid and amusing diaries of 17th-century life, wrote of a service in St Olave's, 'To church where Mr Mills preached, but I know not how. I slept most of the sermon.' A service to commemorate this less than attentive member of the congregation is attended by the Lord Mayor and Sheriffs. It's a popular service, so get there early.

Tube: Tower Hill
Date: on or near 4 June
Time: 1200

EXTRA . . . EXTRA . . . Many victims of the plague were buried in St Olave's churchyard. It was christened 'the churchyard of St Ghastly Grim' by Charles Dickens in *The Uncommercial Traveller*.

CITY OF LONDON FESTIVAL

The festival was first organized in 1962 as a celebration of the City's cultural heritage and aimed in the words of the then Lord Mayor 'to show many things that are beautiful and inspired in the arts – music, verse, tragedy and comedy – in the setting of this our most historic capital'. There's a whole programme of varied events taking place over three weeks in different venues around the City ranging from an arts and crafts fair to piano recitals and poetry readings. While you do have to pay an admission fee for many of the performances, there's also a great deal that is totally free.

Date: July. For full details of events and venues contact: City Arts Trust, Bishopsgate Institute, 230 Bishopsgate, London EC2. Tel: 01-377 0540

EXTRA . . . EXTRA . . . It's well worth making a personal visit to the Bishopsgate Institute to get more information about the Festival – the reference library, which is open to the public, is full of interesting books on London and its history and there's an important collection of London prints and drawings in the lending library.

DOGGETT'S COAT AND BADGE RACE,
Thames (London Bridge, SE1, to Cadogan Pier, SW3)

The prize for the winner of this single-sculling race for Thames Watermen is the Doggett's Coat and Badge – a distinctive scarlet uniform with a huge silver badge. The race is rowed over a distance of 4½ miles from London Bridge to Cadogan Pier. The tradition began in 1714, the idea of Thomas Doggett, a popular Irish actor-comedian. Apparently, Doggett was finding it difficult to find a boat to take him home one stormy night. Then a young waterman eventually rowed him to Chelsea and Doggett was so grateful, he founded this race, open only to first year Freemen of London. You can get a good view if you stand on the Embankment anywhere along the route, but to see the finish head for Albert Bridge, SW3.

Tube: Start: London Bridge
    Finish: Sloane Square, South Kensington
Date: late July
Times: Tel: 01-730 3488 (London Tourist Board and
    Convention Bureau)

EXTRA ... EXTRA ... A poem was written about Thomas Doggett several years after his death which sums up his popularity at the time:

> Tom Doggett, the greatest sly droll in his parts,
> In acting was certain a master of arts;
> A monument left – no herald is fuller –
> His praise is sung yearly by many a sculler.
> Ten thousand years hence if the world last so long
> Tom Doggett will still be the theme of their song.

SWAN UPPING, Thames (Sunbury-on-Thames to Whitchurch)

The swans on the Thames are owned jointly by the Sovereign, the Vintners' Company and the Dyers' Company. This 300-year-old ceremony, which lasts six days with boats leaving from different points each day, is to establish the ownership of the cygnets and to count and mark them. They're identified by the parent swan. If the beak isn't nicked then the swan belongs to the Queen and the cygnets are left unmarked. A Dyers' Company swan has one nick in its beak and a Vintners' Company swan two nicks. When the boats come in sight of Windsor Castle, all the Swan Uppers stand to attention in their boats and, raising their oars, salute 'Her Majesty the Queen, Seigneur of the Swans'.

Date: 3rd week in July
Times: Boats start at different points each day. Contact 01-236 1863 for details.

EXTRA ... EXTRA ... Keep your eyes open for another tradition. Each 'colt', a new boy to Swan Upping, is ducked in the water at some stage. He knows it's coming but has no idea when!

VINTNERS' COMPANY PROCESSION, Upper Thames Street, EC4

Dressed in full traditional costume, members of the Vintners' Company walk from their Hall to the Church of St James's, Garlickhythe, for a special service to celebrate

'Installation Day', the election of a new master. The procession, which lasts only about ten minutes, is headed by the Company's 'tackle porter' (wine porter), wearing a white smock and black silk top hat. He sweeps the path with birch brooms for the members of the Court. This custom dates back to the times when the roads were littered with rubbish and muck. The members of Court carry a nosegay of sweet herbs 'so that their nostrils be not offended by any noxious flavours or other ill-vapours'. It makes a tremendous, and sweet-smelling, sight!

Tube: Blackfriars, Mansion House
Date: 2nd Wednesday in July
Time: procession leaves Vintners' Hall at 1150;
procession leaves St James's, Garlickhythe,
Garlick Hill, EC4, at 1245

EXTRA . . . EXTRA . . . Hugh Herland, Chief Carpenter to Edward III, Richard II and Henry VI, and the designer of Westminster Hall roof, lived at 24–25 Upper Thames Street, EC4.

NOTTING HILL CARNIVAL, Ladbroke Grove and Notting Hill, W11

Move to the music of the steel bands, watch the colourful floats, and marvel at the limbo dancing. Just to be a part of this West Indian carnival is an uplifting experience. It's received a lot of bad publicity in past years, but most people come away wondering what all the talk concerning violence is about. Any fighting seems to be in selected corners while the predominant feeling is one of simply having a good time. The children's Carnival on Sunday is always a fun affair.

Tube: Ladbroke Grove, Notting Hill Gate
Date: August Bank Holiday Sunday and Monday
Time: 1000 onwards

EXTRA . . . EXTRA . . . There's a competition for the best costume on Monday, so make sure you dress the part!

RIDING HORSE PARADE, Rotten Row, Hyde Park, W1

The Riding Horse Parade was first held in 1938 with the aim of raising the standard of the turnout of horses and riders in Rotten Row, a favourite riding ground in central London. There are a whole variety of events with about 50–100 horses and riders taking part and competing for prizes.

Tube: Hyde Park Corner
Date: 1st Sunday in August
Time: 1400 onwards

EXTRA . . . EXTRA . . . Rotten Row is a popular track for riding enthusiasts. It's thought that the name comes from 'route de roi', the 'road of the King', i.e. George II.

CART MARKING, Guildhall Yard, Gresham Street, EC2

This is the annual renewal of licences for City of London street traders. You can watch the Keeper of Guildhall as he marks the carts with the City Arms on the shafts and gives each one a number on a brass plate. This marking dates back to 1681 when the number of carts in the City was limited to 420, but it was only in 1838 that the Keeper of Guildhall was given the duty. (*See also Guildhall, page 42.*)

Tube: Bank, Moorgate, St Paul's, Mansion House
Date: mid-August
Time: Tel: 01-606 3030

EXTRA . . . EXTRA . . . The motto on the City Arms is '*Domine dirige nos*', this means 'O Lord guide us'.

CROMWELL'S DAY, Cromwell Statue, St Margaret Street, SW1

Oliver Cromwell, the great Puritan statesman, died on 3 September 1658, and to pay tribute to him a service is held annually at his statue which stands outside the Palace of Westminster. (*See Houses of Parliament, page 184.*) It's arranged by the Cromwell Association and an address is given by a Cromwellian.

Tube: Westminster
Date: 3 September
Time: 1500

EXTRA . . . EXTRA . . . Cromwell was buried with great dignity on 26 September 1658. However, a few years later, after the restoration of the monarchy, his body was dug up and hanged at Tyburn. Later, the body was cut up and the head placed on a spike above Westminster Hall where it remained until it blew down in 1685. It's said the head is now kept in a box by Cromwell's Suffolk descendants.

ELECTION OF THE LORD MAYOR, Guildhall, Gresham Street, EC2

This is a fine example of the City at its most traditional. The whole process of the election of the Lord Mayor is still surrounded by age-old customs. The Lord Mayor is nominated by the Liverymen of the City, who submit names for a final selection by the Court of Aldermen. All candidates must be Aldermen and must have served as Sheriff. On the actual day of election, the reigning Lord Mayor and the Sheriffs leave Mansion House (*page 50*) and proceed in full ceremony to Guildhall (*page 42*). Here they are met by the Keeper of Guildhall who presents them with nosegays of garden flowers – an ancient protection from the foul-smelling, disease-infected streets. Before the election begins, a service is held in the Church of St Lawrence Jewry-next-Guildhall (*page 58*), Gresham Street, EC2, and attended by the Court of Aldermen, High Officers and the robed masters of all the City Livery Companies. They then walk, posies still in hand, to Guildhall where the Common Cryer and Serjeant-at-Arms officially start the ceremony. Afterwards, the retiring Lord Mayor returns to Mansion House with the Lord Mayor elect in a state coach.

Tube: Bank, Mansion House
Date: 29 September
Tickets: apply in advance to Keeper of Guildhall,
Guildhall, Gresham Street, EC2

EXTRA . . . EXTRA . . . The first Mayor of London was Henry FitzAilwyn who held office from about 1192 until his death in 1212. Three years later King John granted the right to elect a new Mayor each year. The office is now recognized as the highest honour a citizen of London can be given.

HORSEMAN'S SUNDAY, Church of St John and St Michael, Hyde Park Crescent, W2

This service is a relatively new tradition, dating back to 1969, when many local riding stables feared closure and held an open-air service to protest. Some 100 riders and drivers of horses gather for a warming stirrup cup in Radnor Place, W2, and then proceed, led by the Vicar, also on horseback, to the front of the church. It's by no means a peaceful service with the clatter of hooves and general horse guffawing, but it's certainly a spirited one!

Tube: Paddington, Marble Arch
Date: 3rd Sunday in September
Times: meet in Radnor Place at 1130
arrive at Church at 1200

EXTRA . . . EXTRA . . . Walk down to St Mary's Hospital on busy Praed Street, W2. This is where, in a tiny laboratory in September 1928, Alexander Fleming discovered penicillin. Fleming always maintained that it was pure accident: 'It arrived nameless and numberless – all I did was notice it.'

ST MATTHEW'S DAY MARCH, Church of St Sepulchre, Holborn Viaduct, EC4

Although there's not much room in the actual service, you can still watch the procession. Over 300 pupils (boys and girls) of Christ's Hospital School leave the church after the service and march, dressed in their official Tudor-design uniform of blue ankle-length coats, yellow stockings and buckled shoes (hence the nickname 'Blue Coat Boys'), accompanied by the music of the school band, to Mansion House (*page 50*) where the Lord Mayor hands each of them a money gift of freshly minted coins.

Tube: St Paul's
Date: on or near 21 September
Time: Tel: 01-248 1660

EXTRA . . . EXTRA . . . Christ's Hospital, based at Horsham for boys and Hertford for girls, was founded in 1553 by Edward VI as a school for needy children. Among its Old Blue Coat Boys are names such as Samuel Taylor Coleridge, Charles Lamb and Leigh Hunt.

COSTERMONGERS' HARVEST FESTIVAL,
St Martin-in-the-Fields, Trafalgar Square, WC2

The Pearly Kings, Queens, Princes and Princesses from all the London boroughs, dressed in their traditional costumes covered with pearl buttons, are a splendid sight as they gather together in cockney fellowship for a harvest thanksgiving. These 'Pearlies' or Costermongers, to give them their proper title, were originally apple sellers, but due to their flamboyant dress soon became well known locally and used their popularity to help raise money for charity. They're still involved in a great deal of charitable work. At the service, the monarch of each borough brings fruit, flowers and vegetables to be given to the old and poor. The Vicar of St Martin-in-the-Fields (*page 59*) is made an honorary 'Pearly' for the day and wears a stole of pearl buttons.

Tube: Charing Cross
Date: 1st Sunday in October
Time: 1500. For details Tel: 01-930 0089

EXTRA . . . EXTRA . . . The first Costermonger to appear dressed from head to toe in hand-sewn pearl buttons was Henry Croft around 1880. There's a lifesize figure of him at his tomb in St Pancras Cemetery.

HARVEST OF THE SEA THANKSGIVING, St
Mary-at-Hill, Eastcheap, EC3

Although the Billingsgate fish market (*page 179*) has now moved to West India Dock, the Fish Harvest Festival is still held at St Mary-at-Hill, the traditional parish church of Billingsgate. The whole church reeks of fish. Merchants arrange fish of every kind in the porch area and drape nets at the back of the church. The centre pews of the church are reserved for the fish trade but everyone is welcome to sit in the side aisles. After the service, the fish are given to Church Army hostels for the aged in London.

Tube: Monument
Date: 2nd Sunday in October
Times: Tel: 01-626 4184

EXTRA . . . EXTRA . . . The Great Fire of London started from a baker's shop in Pudding Lane, EC3, in 1666, and The Monument was built in 1671–7 to commemorate it. Although you have to pay to climb this fluted column, everyone is at liberty to stand and admire it. The Monument stands 202 feet high and is exactly 202 feet from the shop where the Fire began.

LION SERMON, St Katharine Cree Church, Leadenhall Street, EC3

This service has been held since 1649 and commemorates an exciting escape from death. In 1643 Sir John Gayer, a London merchant who later became Lord Mayor, went on a trading trip to the Levant. Here he lost his fellow travellers and suddenly found himself face to face with a lion. He remembered Daniel and started praying for help. It came, and the lion left him unharmed! Sir John left money for an annual sermon which, although the fund has run out, still continues. The sermon, as you might expect, includes a text from the book of Daniel.

Tube: Bank, Aldgate
Date: 16 October (or the following Monday if this falls at a weekend)
Time: 1305. Tel: 01-283 5733

EXTRA . . . EXTRA . . . There are some curious things uncovered in renovation. Here's a fine example. When the glass in the east window of St Katharine Cree Church was taken down to be cleaned they found an inscription written with a sharp point: 'Thomas Jordan cleaned this window, and damn the job I say – 1815.'

NATIONAL SERVICE FOR SEAFARERS,
St Paul's Cathedral, St Paul's Churchyard, EC4

This service was first held in 1905, on the centenary of the Battle of Trafalgar, and is dedicated to all those people who spend their lives at sea such as the Navy, the Merchant Navy, the Lifeboatmen, fishermen and lighthouse keepers.

The congregation is made up of many smartly uniformed officers and trainees who make everyone welcome. Before and after the service a Royal Marines Band plays. During the service, you sing along with a choir made up of Naval Schools from all over the country. (*See also St Paul's Cathedral, pages 64*).

Tube: St Paul's
Date: Wednesday nearest to 21 October

Tickets: apply before 12 September to The Hon.
Secretary, Annual National Service for
Seafarers, St Michael Paternoster Royal,
College Hill, EC4, tel: 01-248 5202

EXTRA . . . EXTRA . . . The service is always held in St
Paul's Cathedral because this is where Lord Nelson is
buried. You'll find a memorial to him, side by side with
one to the Duke of Wellington, in the Crypt.

PUNCH AND JUDY FESTIVAL, Covent Garden
Piazza, Covent Garden, WC2

Punch and Judy, a violent pair of puppets who delight
both adults and children alike, have their own annual
festival. Samuel Pepys watched the first Punch and Judy
show on 9 May 1662 in the covered doorway of St Paul's
Church. The Punch and Judy Fellowship also hold a
festival on the piazza in Covent Garden on a Sunday in
October.

Tube: Covent Garden, Leicester Square
Date: October. Tel: 01-802 4656 for details

EXTRA . . . EXTRA . . . Parliamentary elections used to
take place on the same site, in front of St Paul's Church.

TRAFALGAR DAY, Trafalgar Square, WC2

Trafalgar Day is one of the most important dates in the naval calendar. Dinners and celebrations to commemorate Nelson's great victory in 1805 are held in naval headquarters all over the country. These are private affairs. However, you can join in the Trafalgar Sunday Commemoration Service and wreath-laying ceremony at the base of Nelson's Column in Trafalgar Square (*page 68*). It's always a well-attended service.

Tube: Charing Cross
Date: Sunday nearest to 21 October
Time: 1100

EXTRA . . . EXTRA . . . If you'd like to join in Nelson's prayer, given before the Battle of Trafalgar, the words are: 'May the Great God whom I worship grant to my country, and for the benefit of Europe in general, a great and glorious victory; and may no misconduct in anyone tarnish it; and may humanity after victory be the predominant feature in the British Fleet. For myself, individually, I commit my life to Him that made me, and may His blessing alight on my endeavours for serving my country faithfully. To Him I resign myself and the just cause which He entrusted me to defend.'

STATE OPENING OF PARLIAMENT, House of Lords, Palace of Westminster, SW1

Although the general public aren't allowed into the actual ceremony, you can watch the Queen as she arrives and departs in the Irish State Coach, accompanied by the Duke of Edinburgh and attended by the Household Cavalry. She leaves from Buckingham Palace (*page 36*), proceeds along the Mall and through Horse Guards Parade (*page 46*) to the House of Lords. As she enters, a gun is fired. Inside she reads a speech announcing the policies and programme of the Government for the new session of Parliament. Get there early to catch a glimpse of the action. (*See also Houses of Parliament, page 184.*)

Tube: Westminster
Date: late October/early November, or when a new
      Government comes to power. Tel: 01-219 4272
Times: procession leaves Buckingham Palace at 1040
      arrives House of Lords at 1100

EXTRA . . . EXTRA . . . The Crown travels separately – in Queen Alexandra's Coach – and leaves Buckingham Palace for the House of Lords at about 1030. It's proudly guarded by the Queen's Bargemaster and four Royal Watermen.

ADMISSION OF THE LORD MAYOR,
Guildhall, Gresham Street, EC2

This is the day when the new Lord Mayor begins his year of office. With full ceremony the Lord Mayor is handed the symbols of office – the Sword and Mace, the Crystal Sceptre, the Seal, and the 16th-century City Purse. Then the two Lord Mayors, old and new, exchange their seats – a process which takes place in total silence and is called, quite naturally, the 'Silent Exchange'. (*See also Guildhall, page 42.*)

Tube: Bank, Moorgate, St Paul's, Mansion House
Date: 2nd Friday in November
Tickets: apply in writing to Keeper of Guildhall,
            Guildhall, Gresham Street, London EC2

EXTRA . . . EXTRA . . . On Admission Day the Lord Mayor wears a robe of violet silk. The Lord Mayor has a different robe for each occasion but by far the most splendid is the Coronation robe made of crimson velvet with a train edged with gold lace. But there is only one hat – a tricorn trimmed with a black ostrich plume.

CHRISTMAS LIGHTS, Oxford Street and Regent Street, W1

The lights along these two streets are always turned on by a member of the Royal Family or a famous personality. They give a festive air to two of the most popular shopping streets in London.

Tube: Oxford Circus, Piccadilly Circus
Date: from mid-November until 6 January
Times: Tel: 01-730 3488 (London Tourist Board and
          Convention Bureau)

EXTRA . . . EXTRA . . . Hamley's, at 200 Regent Street, W1, is the largest toy shop in the world with 45,000 square feet of selling space. It's at its best at Christmas when you can spend a whole day playing with the toys and watching the demonstrations.

FIREWORK NIGHT

Huge bonfires are built in the London parks and open spaces to commemorate the Gunpowder Plot of 1605, when Guy Fawkes and his friends tried unsuccessfully to blow up the Houses of Parliament (*page 184*). Not all the displays are free but many are, and even if you can't get to an actual firework show you can still enjoy the rockets as they light up the sky.

Date: 5 November
Time: Tel: 01-730 3488 (London Tourist Board and Convention Bureau)

EXTRA . . . EXTRA . . . Since the failure of the Gunpowder Plot, it has been a tradition that before every State Opening of Parliament (*page 228*) the vaults beneath are searched by Yeomen of the Guard wearing full uniform.

LONDON TO BRIGHTON VETERAN CAR RUN, Hyde Park Corner, W1, to Marine Parade, Brighton, Sussex

This is the oldest competitive motoring event in history, first held in November 1896. It commemorates 'Emancipation Day' when it was no longer necessary for a man with a red flag to walk in front of the new 'horseless carriages'. There are 300 entrants who come from all over the world with their spotless veteran cars all wearing the full garb. Get to the start early as there are always plenty of people watching, or cheer them on from anywhere along the main A23 to Brighton. (*See also London to Brighton Bike Race, page 212.*)

Tube: Hyde Park Corner
Date: 1st Sunday in November
Time: run begins 0800–0900. Tel: 01-235 8601

EXTRA . . . EXTRA . . . What is a veteran car? In case you're confused, veteran cars were made before 1904. The Edwardian period cars date from 1905 to 1918, and vintage cars from 1919 to 1930. After then they're classed as post-vintage.

LORD MAYOR'S SHOW

The City of London is taken over for a day with colourful floats, street dancing and much merriment. This is the new Lord Mayor's day. In a gilded coach, drawn by a team of six Shires from Whitbread's City brewery stables, the Lord Mayor travels from Guildhall (*page 42*) to the Royal Courts of Justice (*page 191*) to make a statutory declaration of office before the Lord Chief Justice and Judges of the Queen's Bench Division. The Lord Mayor's procession usually leaves Guildhall around mid-morning, stops at Mansion House (*page 50*) to take a salute, and then proceeds along Cheapside, Ludgate Hill and Fleet Street to the Royal Courts of Justice, returning via

Victoria Embankment and Queen Victoria Street to Mansion House. You can join in the fun anywhere along the route.

Tube: Bank, Mansion House, St Paul's, Temple
Date: 2nd Saturday in November
Times: leaves Guildhall at 1130
       leaves Royal Courts of Justice at 1300

EXTRA . . . EXTRA . . . The Shires have been supplied by Whitbread's City brewery stables since 1955. Samuel Whitbread's original King's Head Brewery was founded in 1742 on the site of what is now The King's Head pub on the corner of Whitecross Road and Chiswell Street, EC1.

REMEMBRANCE SUNDAY, The Cenotaph, Whitehall, SW1

Whitehall is lined with mourning crowds as everyone gathers to pay silent tribute to the men of all three Services and Allied Forces who gave their lives for their country. Detachments of the Armed Forces and ex-servicemen and women, able-bodied and wounded, all come to remember the dead. The Queen arrives at the Cenotaph at 1059 and a minute later a gun is fired by the King's Troop of the Royal Horse Artillery from Horse Guards Parade. This is the start of two minutes' silence which ends with the firing of another gun. The Buglers of the Royal Marines then sound *The Last Post* and the Queen steps forward to lay the first wreath of poppies by The Cenotaph. Other wreaths are laid by members of the

Royal Family and representatives from the Government, Commonwealth Governments and the Services, all to the music of a funeral march. Finally, the Bishop of London takes a short service of Remembrance. It's a most moving experience and one which leaves you feeling quite emotionally drained. Do get there early though. (*See also Royal British Legion Poppy Factory, page 190.*)

Tube: Westminster
Date: 2nd Sunday in November
Time: 1030

EXTRA . . . EXTRA . . . The Cenotaph, the national memorial to the dead of World Wars I and II, was designed in 1919 by Sir Edwin Lutyens as an outward symbol of inward grief. The inscription reads 'To the Glorious Dead'.

CAROLS AT WESTMINSTER ABBEY,
Westminster Abbey, Westminster, SW1

Christmas at Westminster Abbey (*page 70*) doesn't begin until 25 December – the anniversary of the birth of Christ. Nor do the Abbey's carol services. To be among the congregation at one of their carol services is a real pleasure. There's no commercialism here and you can enjoy the true warmth and spirit of Christmas.

Tube: Westminster, St James's Park
Date: 26, 27, 28 December
Time: 1500. Tel: 01-222 5152

EXTRA . . . EXTRA . . . The alleged author of one of the most popular Christmas carols, 'While shepherds watch'd their flocks by night', Nahum Tate (1652–1715), is buried in the churchyard of St George the Martyr, Borough High Street, SE1 (*see page 56*).

CHRISTMAS TREE, Trafalgar Square, WC2

Each year the citizens of Oslo, Norway, give the citizens of London a Christmas tree which is erected in Trafalgar Square (*page 68*) and decorated with white lights. Everyone is welcome to come and admire the tree and to join in the charity Christmas carol services held every evening up to Christmas Eve.

Tube: Charing Cross, Leicester Square
Date: early December

EXTRA . . . EXTRA . . . The Christmas tree is thought to have originated in Germany. Legend has it that Martin Luther was walking through the woods one night when he saw the light glistening on the trees and hit on the idea of putting up a candlelit tree for his children.

DICKENS'S DRIVE, Doughty Street, WC1, to St Peter's Church, Eaton Square, SW1

It's a great spectacle – a party dressed in Dickensian costume, riding in a stagecoach drawn by four silver-grey horses. You can watch them as they set out from Dickens's House and drive, stopping for refreshment *en route*, to St Peter's Church for an evening service and traditional reading from *A Christmas Carol*.

Tube: Russell Square
Date: mid-December. Tel: 01-567 7510
Times: leaves Doughty Street at 1445
       arrives at Church at 1830

EXTRA . . . EXTRA . . . Charles Dickens moved to 48 Doughty Street, WC1, in 1836, and lived there for nearly three years. It was here that he wrote *Oliver Twist*, finished *Pickwick Papers* and started *Barnaby Rudge*. It was also here that his wife's sister, Mary Hogarth, died in May 1837, a tragic loss that deeply affected Dickens.

NEW YEAR CELEBRATIONS, Trafalgar Square, WC2

As Big Ben strikes midnight on 31 December each year, London bursts into life to welcome the New Year. Trafalgar Square is a rather undignified crush of people with a band of brave policemen trying to keep some sort of order. If you don't mind being pushed about by the crowds and fancy the idea of a late-night dip in one of the fountains, then this is the place to be.

Tube: Charing Cross, Leicester Square
Date: 31 December
Time: 2100 onwards

EXTRA . . . EXTRA . . . You can hear the chimes of Big Ben announcing the New Year on radio and television. Big Ben was first broadcast on New Year's Eve, 1923.

CHAPTER EIGHT
Walks

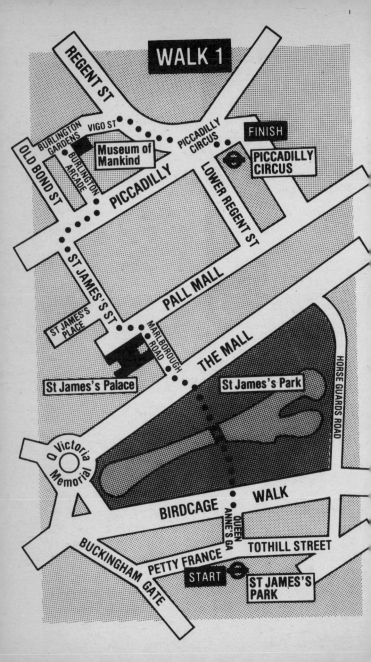

WALK 1 ST JAMES'S PARK–ST JAMES'S PALACE–PICCADILLY–BURLINGTON ARCADE–MUSEUM OF MANKIND–PICCADILLY CIRCUS

Get off the tube at St James's Park, walk through Queen Anne's Gate, and cross busy Birdcage Walk to **St James's Park** (*page 168*). Leave the park through the large gates which lead on to the Mall (there are some quite reasonable toilets here). Walk up Marlborough Road, passing St James's Palace on the left. The palace, which is not open to the public, became the official residence of the sovereign after Whitehall burned down in 1698; however, Queen Victoria moved the court to **Buckingham Palace** (*page 36*) on her accession in 1837. At the top of Marlborough Road turn left, then almost immediately right into St James's Street, noting as you do so the Tudor Gatehouse or Clock Tower belonging to St James's Palace. Walk up St James's Street, taking a brief excursion into St James's Place to see the house (number 4) where Chopin lived and from where he went to give his last public performance at the **Guildhall** (*page 42*) in 1848. At the top of St James's Street turn right into Piccadilly. After you've finished admiring the window displays of Fortnum and Mason, cross the road and continue window-shopping in exquisite Burlington Arcade. Built in 1819, this covered promenade retains its Regency atmosphere. As you come out of the north end of the arcade turn right; immediately on your right is the **Museum of Mankind** (*page 122*). When you come out of the museum continue walking down Burlington Gardens to Regent Street. Piccadilly Circus tube station is now only a few minutes' walk away – which will be a considerable relief to your feet!

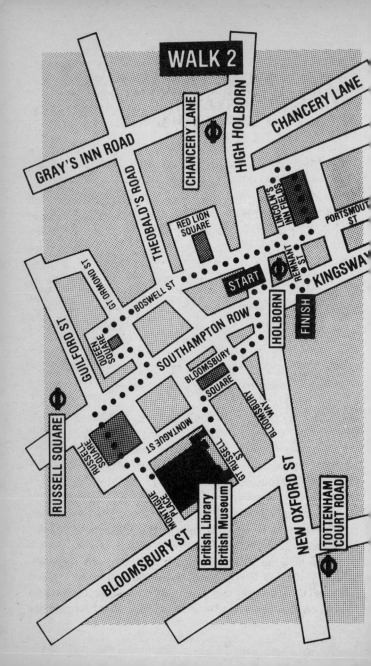

WALK 2   BRITISH MUSEUM–RUSSELL SQUARE–LINCOLN'S INN FIELDS–SIR JOHN SOANE'S MUSEUM–OLD CURIOSITY SHOP

Start your walk at Holborn tube station. Cross busy High Holborn then turn right into equally busy Southampton Row. Walk a short way up Southampton Row, passing on your right Catton Street and Fisher Street, until you reach the Central School of Art and Design (*see Degree and Diploma Exhibitions, page 19*). Here, once again braving the traffic, cross Southampton Row and turn into pretty Sicilian Avenue. Cut through this stylish pedestrian avenue to Bloomsbury Square. Leaving the square by its north exit turn left into Great Russell Street; on your right is the monumental **British Museum** (*page 99*). The museum is huge, wonderful and very tiring! When you've seen all you can manage, leave by its north exit into Montague Place. Walk a few hundred yards east to **Russell Square** (*page 168*) – a good place to rest (you'll need to by now!) and have a picnic lunch. Leave Russell Square by the gateway which leads back onto Southampton Row and walk a short way south to Cosmo Place which is on your left. At the end of this short passage is Queen Square – a pleasant place to linger for a while, particularly in the summer when the flower-beds blaze with colour. You're now completely surrounded by hospitals! To the south of the square is Boswell Street; walk down it. Now cross Theobald's Road, walk down Drake Street (noticing 17th-century Red Lion Square which takes its name from a nearby tavern), and at the bottom cross High Holborn. Immediately in front of you is a narrow alleyway called Little Turnstile, which widens into Gate Street, which in turn leads to **Lincoln's Inn Fields** (*page 163*). At number

13 is the **Sir John Soane's Museum** (*page 135*) and nearby, in Portsmouth Street, is the Old Curiosity Shop. Built in 1567, it's a fine example of Tudor architecture; it also houses a few Charles Dickens mementoes. If you've any energy left, to the east is the City – full of treasures – but, more likely, you'll want to make your way home. Retrace your steps up Portsmouth Street and turn left into Remnant Street, emerging onto Kingsway. Holborn tube station is just a few minutes' walk to your right.

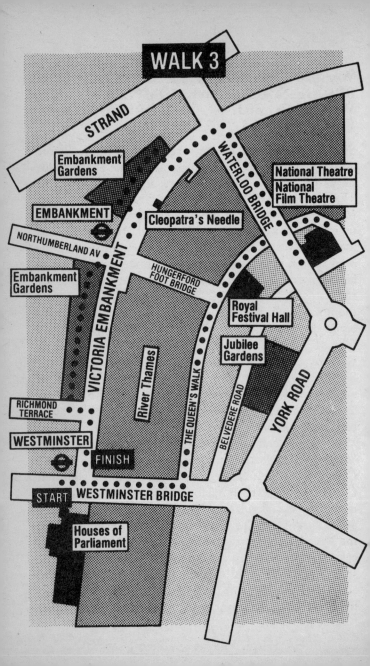

WALK 3

STRAND

Embankment Gardens

EMBANKMENT

NORTHUMBERLAND AV

Embankment Gardens

VICTORIA EMBANKMENT

Cleopatra's Needle

WATERLOO BRIDGE

National Theatre

National Film Theatre

HUNGERFORD FOOT BRIDGE

Royal Festival Hall

Jubilee Gardens

River Thames

THE QUEEN'S WALK

BELVEDERE ROAD

YORK ROAD

RICHMOND TERRACE

WESTMINSTER

FINISH

START WESTMINSTER BRIDGE

Houses of Parliament

WALK 3 WESTMINSTER–WESTMINSTER BRIDGE–SOUTH BANK COMPLEX– WATERLOO BRIDGE–VICTORIA EMBANKMENT GARDENS

Start your walk at Westminster tube station. Before crossing Westminster Bridge, stand a while at the statue of Queen Boadicea and admire the view across the Thames. Notice the 'Golden Eagle', the Royal Air Force Memorial on Victoria Embankment, and the river boats taking passengers to Kew, Richmond, Hampton Court and Greenwich. Walk over the bridge and turn left at the South Bank Lion which looks mournfully towards Lambeth. You're in The Queen's Walk, named to commemorate Queen Elizabeth II's Silver Jubilee in 1977. Notice the poems and witty ditties carved in the paving stones along the walkway. On your right is County Hall, and then a few minutes on to your right you'll come to **Jubilee Gardens** (*page 159*). Next you have the whole of the South Bank complex to explore, with free entertainment at the **Royal Festival Hall** (*page 28*) and the **National Theatre** (*page 23*). If you've time, sit on one of the many benches overlooking the Thames.

To complete the circle, cross Waterloo Bridge (*page 86*), with the spectacular view of the dome of **St Paul's Cathedral** (*page 64*) on your right, and to your left Cleopatra's Needle on Victoria Embankment. Turn left into **Victoria Embankment Gardens** (*page 170*), looking at the many statues as you walk through. On your right is the back entrance to the Savoy, one of London's most celebrated hotels. As you approach Embankment tube station you'll see the bandstand where they hold band concerts in the summer (*page 25*). Continue across Northumberland Avenue and into the gardens on the other side. Then turn left down Richmond Terrace and into Victoria Embankment. You'll see **Big Ben** (*page 34*) and the **Houses of Parliament** (*page 184*) directly in front of you. And now you're back again at Westminster tube station.

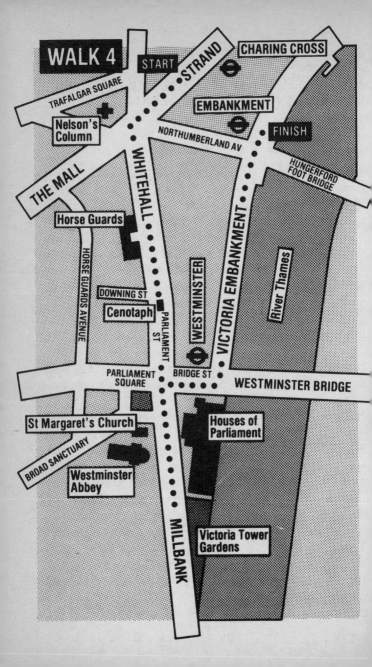

WALK 4 TRAFALGAR SQUARE–HORSE GUARDS–CENOTAPH–ST MARGARET'S –WESTMINSTER ABBEY–VICTORIA TOWER GARDENS–PALACE OF WESTMINSTER–BIG BEN

Start your walk at **Trafalgar Square** (*page 68*). Charing Cross and Leicester Square are the nearest tube stations. Stop to look at Nelson's Column and notice to your right the Admiralty Arch and the spectacular view of the Mall and **Buckingham Palace** (*page 36*). But don't walk down the Mall. Instead take the Whitehall road. This is packed with interest on either side. First, on your right, you'll come to **Horse Guards** (*page 46*) with the Queen's Life Guards outside. On the opposite side is Banqueting House. Further along is Downing Street where the Prime Minister lives at Number 10. Walk on a little way to The Cenotaph, the memorial to those who lost their lives defending the country, and continue to Parliament Square, past the statue of Sir Winston Churchill, and into St Margaret Street with the **Palace of Westminster**, the official title for the **Houses of Parliament** (*page 184*), to your left. But first go to the church of **St Margaret's** (*page 59*), the parish church of the House of Commons, which is opposite. And on to **Westminster Abbey** (*page 70*) next to the church. Remember that the **Westminster Abbey Gardens** (*page 173*) are open to the public on Thursdays. The gardens lead on to Great College Street at the south side of the Abbey. Cross Millbank and you're in **Victoria Tower Gardens** (*page 170*), offering lovely views across the Thames to Lambeth. The Palace of Westminster, with the Victoria Tower and clock tower containing **Big Ben** (*page 34*), overlooks the gardens. And this is your next port of call. Nearby is Westminster tube station. If you

wish you can continue back up Whitehall to Charing
Cross tube station or walk along Victoria Embankment
and through the **Victoria Embankment Gardens** (*page
170*) to Embankment tube station.

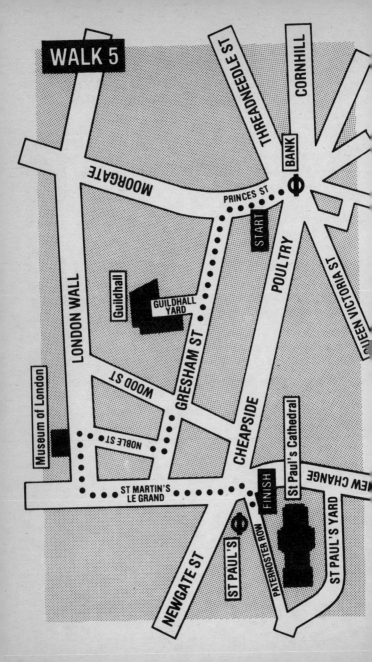

WALK 5 BANK–GUILDHALL–LONDON WALL–LONDON MUSEUM–ST PAUL'S CATHEDRAL

Get off the tube at Bank and walk up Princess Street, noting the site of the General Letter Office (1653–66). Turn left into Gresham Street and on your right is **Guildhall, Guildhall Library** (*page 108*), and **Clockmakers' Company Museum** (*page 102*); also worth a visit is **St Lawrence Jewry-next-Guildhall** (*page 58*). By now you'll need a rest so make for the Garden of St John Zachary on the corner of Gresham Street and Noble Street. This tiny garden is on the site of a church destroyed by the fire of 1666. It has lots of seats, but as it's rather ugly don't sit too long; instead walk on up Noble Street to **London Wall** (*page 49*) and the **Museum of London** (*page 121*). This excellent museum will probably take at least 2–3 hours to visit so allow yourself plenty of time. When you've learnt everything you want to know about London's history and leave the museum, walk down Aldersgate Street and St Martin's-le-Grand to St Paul's tube station. If you can summon up just a bit more energy, pop into **St Paul's Cathedral** (*page 64*) – it's breathtaking every time.

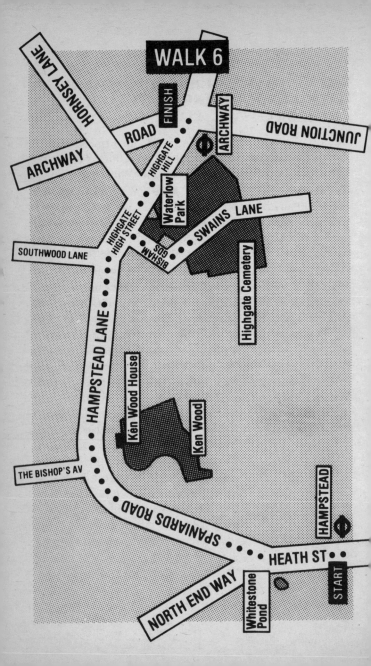

WALK 6   HAMPSTEAD–WHITESTONE POND–KENWOOD–HIGHGATE CEMETERY–WATERLOW PARK–WHITTINGTON STONE

Start your walk at Hampstead tube station. Turn right into Heath Street and follow it up to Whitestone Pond. At weekends in the summer there are **Open-Air Art Exhibitions** (*page 24*) in Heath Street. Turn right at Jack Straw's Castle and into Spaniards Road. **Hampstead Heath** (*page 156*) is on either side of you, but for now just admire the views – the Heath is worth saving for another day. Walk up past the Spaniards Inn on your left and into Hampstead Lane. You'll come to **Kenwood** (*page 115*) on your right with its beautifully landscaped park. If you take a slight detour before going to Kenwood, and turn left into The Bishops Avenue, you'll see how 'the other half lives'. The houses along this road are more like mini-palaces. Continue along Hampstead Lane to Highgate High Street, and into Bisham Gardens. Turn left into Swains Lane and you'll come to the entrances to **Highgate Cemetery** (*page 45*) and **Waterlow Park** (*page 172*) – both well worth a visit. Leave Waterlow Park by the entrance on Highgate High Street and do a little window-shopping in Highgate Village. Walk down Highgate Hill, past the impressive St Joseph's Church and Whittington Hospital, and down to the Whittington Stone, which is at the foot of the hill. This stone, capped with a black cat, is a memorial to Dick Whittington and his good works. Yes, he really did exist and was Sheriff in 1393 and Lord Mayor of London in 1397, 1406 and 1420. Facing you now is Archway tube station where the walk ends.

Index

Regional books in paperback from Grafton Books

Chris Barber
Mysterious Wales (illustrated)   £2.50 ☐

Brian J. Bailey
Lakeland Walks and Legends (illustrated)   £1.50 ☐

Tom Weir
Weir's Way (illustrated)   £2.95 ☐

David Daiches
Edinburgh (illustrated)   £1.95 ☐
Glasgow (illustrated)   £3.95 ☐

Peter Somerville-Large
Dublin (illustrated)   £2.25 ☐

Frank Delaney
James Joyce's Odyssey (illustrated)   £2.95 ☐

Mary Cathcart Borer
London Walks and Legends (illustrated)   £1.95 ☐

Mary Peplow and Debra Shipley
London for Free   £2.50 ☐

To order direct from the publisher just tick the titles you want
and fill in the order form.   HB1281

All these books are available at your local bookshop or newsagent, or can be ordered direct from the publisher.

To order direct from the publishers just tick the titles you want and fill in the form below.

Name _____

Address _____

Send to:
Grafton Cash Sales
PO Box 11, Falmouth, Cornwall TR10 9EN.

Please enclose remittance to the value of the cover price plus:

UK 60p for the first book, 25p for the second book plus 15p per copy for each additional book ordered to a maximum charge of £1.90.

BFPO 60p for the first book, 25p for the second book plus 15p per copy for the next 7 books, thereafter 9p per book.

Overseas including Eire £1.25 for the first book, 75p for second book and 28p for each additional book.

Grafton Books reserve the right to show new retail prices on covers, which may differ from those previously advertised in the text or elsewhere.